Nancy Wilson Ross
One of the first two books she
edited when she went from
Random House to Simon
& Schuster

from "Nan Talese

In hoc mundo me extra me nihil agere posse . . .

Geulincx
Ethica

MUNDOME

•

by
A.G. Mojtabai

•

Simon and Schuster
New York

SBN 671-21731-3
Library of Congress Catalog Card Number: 73-20699
Designed by Elizabeth Woll
Manufactured in the United States of America
By American Book–Stratford Press Inc.

2 3 4 5 6 7 8 9 10

To "Mosquito," *to* Sid—
and
most especially
to Henrietta Gilden

Author's Note

Mundome is a deliberately ungrammatical construction, a forced juxtaposition of words that cannot fuse without some connective of action or relation.

MUNDOME

●

WHEN I THINK of our library I think of nothing less than the archive of the human estate, the house of the memory of man, and more than a house, memory itself, and more than memory, the slow cess of the spirit: vanity and devotion, illusion, and the martyred rose of prophecy—torn, yet living still. "*Excrementum spiritus,*" says Arragan-Horgan. We take it all in.

We take them all in: the cranks, the scholars ungowned, the weary, the sick. We call them all, without distinction, "readers." Only last week, one of our readers died over his prop, the *Encyclopaedia Britannica,* a section on the life of the salmon. We didn't know until closing time, and by then his fingers were blue. It was a clean death. He was an old man and died naturally as old men die. He died of attrition.

Many of our readers come in off the streets just to

get warm, or to snatch a bit of sleep, or to be close to people without having to pay a fare, people with nowhere to go, nearly all of them sober. They deposit a layer of misery, like silt, over the tables and chairs. They bleed copiously over the white pages of the books.

And the librarians? Are we votaries, or mice, or cashiers, behind our wickets, inside these dim enclosures? Refugees all, from one thing or another, all are taken in. Musicians out of work, expatriates, fags, unpublished poets, brooders, dreamers, keepers of the grail, the walking stillborn: the never-would-be's, the almost-was—all clerks to you. Lonely as lighthouse keepers, we have a special feeling for books. Books, to us, are friends and lovers and absent children.

Knowing our ways as well as I do, imagine how shattered I was when Mr. MacFinster, my division chief, called me into his office to announce the arrival of an efficiency expert.

"When?" I asked, for lack of something better to say.

"Soon! Soon!" he replied on a rising note.

"How soon exactly—in the next few minutes? Tomorrow? In a week? A month or two?"

"Frankly, I don't know." MacFinster tried to smile. It wasn't much of a success: the paint flaked. He

12

wiped the crumbs from the corners of his lips. Then he spread out his handkerchief and studied the border, the absence of a border, the eyelet embroidery of an initial. It was "G" with flourishes or tendrils. The detail struck me because G isn't his initial, unless he has a secret one, and it couldn't have been his handkerchief anyway because it reeked of gardenias.

"You'd better look to your statistics, Mr. Henken," he said with a wave of his hanky in my direction. It was as heady as springtime.

"My statistics . . ." I repeated.

I returned to my desk. From there, *sotto voce*, I passed on the word to Arragan-Horgan, Simon Sandowski, Tom Malaniffe, to Ruthie, Mary and Sue, my peers and compatriots. Only Tom hadn't heard rumors or guessed something alien, fearful, in the offing. Somehow I'm always nearly the last to pick up what's common knowledge—why is this?

Because I'm an uncommon fellow.

My desk was completely littered, only here and there an inch of pea-green blotter showing. It was an obvious target of criticism and I decided to begin putting my affairs in order with some simple housekeeping.

There is one drawer on the bottom lefthand side which I've never been able to open. I found it wedged tight when I arrived on the job some two years back. Arragan-Horgan and I started work on the same morning. We tossed coins for desks, having no preferences.

One desk was placed in the line of open windows, was pleasant in summer and bracing, at best, in winter; the other desk—mine, it turned out—was placed in a warm but stuffy corner, facing a stricken wall of mottled institutional green.

It occurred to me only now how much easier it would be if I could simply sweep some of the clutter off the top of my desk into the drawer I had never used. Tugging at the handle gave no result. I had tried that before. It was jammed. I would have called the locksmith, except for the fact that there was no lock.

So I had to make do. I stacked the papers into neat piles, discarding wherever I could. There were a few memos of no great importance I wanted to keep. I decided to stuff them under the blotter.

When I lifted the blotter, a piece of heavy paper fell out. It turned out to be a sketch, a caricature of MacFinster and a very fair likeness, for I recognized him at once. He had a monocle screwed into his left eye. He was bare to the waist; his chest was smooth. He was wearing knickers and his legs were exposed from the knees down, terminating in metal cuffs round the ankles and, instead of feet, little wheels, one on each leg, like sofa casters. The sketch was signed: Ernest Co— I couldn't make out the last name; the end letters simply collapsed, sloped down into nothingness. I figured it was four letters. Something like Cook. Cole? Cord? Or maybe was it five— Corey? There was no telling.

14

The sketch amused me, cheered me in a way. I carefully replaced it, farther back under the blotter, where it wouldn't fall out again. Later, I asked around for news of Ernest Co—.

Tom was too new, but Simon remembered.

"Ernie—Ernie Coke, you mean? The guy that sat at your desk before you? Why? Was there something to know? Nothing special that I noticed. Didn't get along with MacFinster. Nothing special in that. Called him MacFinicky, the tight-lipped and tight-assed. Well, that's hardly a revelation. What else? He had a kind of flair for words, Ernie did. Lots do. Nothing unusual in that, either. Said he wanted to be a writer and was only marking time here till he struck it big. Well, he didn't strike it big, he didn't even click. I don't think he sold a page, or even got a letter to the editor printed in some rag. So—what else can I tell you? Peculiar sense of humor. He used to say that his bum was plaque-shaped, not rounded, and by such a sign you could tell a man of letters. No loonier than the rest of us, only he was louder. Used to broadcast everything he thought. Like every time he had to go to the john he'd announce it—to the whole room. Odd? That's pretty odd, I guess. At the end, he was talking to himself all the time. Loud. Man, it was loud. Like he wanted to make sure we heard every word. Like he wanted to provoke somebody—or maybe it was to drown out something—voices in his head or something, because it sounded like answers to questions nobody was asking. Sometimes it was a scream, really funny, it was a struggle keeping a straight face. We had to keep plugging away, acting deaf. Once in a while, Sandy would split at the seams. But then it got so it wasn't so funny anymore—you know—it got pretty personal.

"But I've seen some real lulus in this room, and one or two at your desk that'd make Ernie look humdrum. What's up, Richard? Why the sudden interest?"

I couldn't say.

By noon it was hard to sit still. Meg would have arrived by eleven if all went well. Was all going well? I kept turning to the clock on the wall. It moved in spasms; at five minute intervals there'd be a snapping sound, and the minute hand would jerk, the hour hand fidget. I hung on the delivery of the minute hand: promise, parcel, promise— It was impossible to work, under the circumstances.

I decided to leave at lunchtime.

When I told Arragan-Horgan that I wasn't feeling well and was leaving for the rest of the day, he said under his breath, "Cop-out. That's what I call a bold stroke. You're in for a three-day weekend, it so happens."

Two-and-a-half, but I didn't deny it.

I told MacFinster, who nodded absently. I'm not sure he registered what I was saying. I glanced back once over my shoulder at him. He was sitting behind his glass partition in the same position as before, busily donning and doffing his handkerchief, rolled up to form a cone, now a cap, now a cape for his thumb. Obviously deep in thought. Once he looked up but past me, clear through me.

I felt better when I passed beyond the lions, tame as lapdogs, that guard the library door, better as I wove past the lanes of pedestrians moving bumper to bumper. I entered the park. The municipal air was rank. The pollution level was "unsafe," worse than yesterday's "unsatisfactory." I had heard it on the radio: they were beginning to give the ratings along with the weather every morning.

In spite of the air, when I left the bus, I felt better still. I put one foot in front of the other with a sense of riches.

"Is anybody there?" I asked as I opened the door. That's my standard greeting.

Does anybody care? came the usual echo.

Meg was sitting alone at the dining-room table. Her hands were outstretched on the oilcloth, and her eyes remained fixed on her hands. Although she's over

17

thirty and in spite of all she's been through, Meg still looked no more than fourteen, not a day more; she looked like a girl who had just reached puberty—and that barely, her face clear and childlike, her mouth a perfect pout, her eyes water blue, reflecting, not remembering. But around her eyes there was the unmistakable residue of ash, some remembering.

"I'm home," I said.

She shrugged her shoulders as if to say, I can see that for myself. And what of it?

"I came home to take you out for a walk. It's beautiful out."

Miss Kay entered. She was not in uniform.

"Nice day?" she put in. "I believe it's pouring out. You call that nice?"

I glanced down at myself. The rain was still fresh and gleaming on my shoulder and sleeve; there was even something of a puddle under my feet to corroborate Miss Kay's assertion. And my hair was wet; I had forgotten my hat.

"Why, so it must be—raining," I conceded. "When it stops, I'm going to take Meg out for some exercise."

"Suit yourself," said Miss Kay.

"I think Meg would like a walk," I presumed.

"Speak for yourself," Miss Kay cautioned.

But of course Meg sat mute throughout our little discussion.

"Wouldn't you, Meg?" I persisted.

"Wouldn't you Meg what? You're insane, that goes without saying," said Meg, staring at the wall.

Naturally, I laughed.

I dismissed Miss Kay for a couple of hours. She was all too eager to be released. As a parting shot, she tossed the *Post* in my direction. "Why don't you read her the paper, the comics or the crosswords. That way *neither* of you gets bored. Get the idea?"

Did I detect sarcasm?

I fixed deviled-ham sandwiches for lunch, cutting them into eighths. Meg has not used her hands in twelve years; she chose not to use them at the beginning, and now she is even losing the power to manipulate them should she want to use them again. They are the hands of an icon; the skin films over ivory tapers of bone. I put—forced, to be exact—the bread between the thumb and trunk fingers of Meg's left hand, where the contraction has begun. She must have been hungry, because she raised her hand to her mouth under her own power and swallowed the tidbits in lumps without much chewing. She even swept over the table with her open right hand, making a sandpaper sound, scouring for crumbs. I curved her hand around her glass of juice; the only help I gave her was in supporting the bottom of her glass. The effect was almost as if Meg were feeding herself. More of this day by day, I thought, and Meg *will* be feeding herself. I'll see to it. It won't be easy, but I mean to keep at her.

It was a long, painstaking lunch and well past two o'clock before I cleared away the dishes. I must have been thinking through Meg's every motion, straining to inhabit her body, for I felt completely drained. I decided we had better sit a while before venturing out.

I opened up the newspaper and began reading aloud. Meg sat on the sofa facing me. With the turning of each fresh page, I repeated the date at the top. It's the first thing they ask before they admit you to ————. The date is very important, the name and the number attached to the day. It's a charm against ————. We try not to say those words in this house.

It was late afternoon, well past four, when I looked up next. Meg was gone, quite gone. She must have gotten up so quietly that I hadn't noticed. The living room was gray in the half-spent light.

It's important for Meg to be up and active. That was my understanding when I was granted permission to take her home. I went after her.

I found her standing in front of the mirror mounted on her wardrobe door. I never liked that mirror; it is coffin-shaped. How long Meg had been standing in front of it, in it, was anyone's guess. I shook her roughly by the shoulder. Her shoulder was as fickle as fabric between my fingers, so thin had she become.

"We're going out for the walk I promised you," I announced.

She surprised me by snapping to, a soldier at the ready.

I brought her raincoat and dressed her.

"Now, Meg—let's be on our way."

It was such slow and heavy going, I felt as if I were dragging a full platoon after me.

By the time we made it to the foyer, we were both overheated. I had made the mistake of putting on my own raincoat before dressing Meg in order to set an example, and also to remind her of the next activity on the agenda. She needs constant reminding; that's to be my role for the present. Sweet dream of reason . . . I have large hopes.

Soon I was drenched with effort. She wilted backwards. Holding and leading her hands, I urged her on. It must have looked like a dance of supplication. The door at the end of the corridor seemed to recede at the same rate as the speed of our approach: a prize, always just out of reach.

Finally I got sick of straining. Motion made so painfully explicit, motion so assiduously, so minutely willed became at last an interminable division, a third to go, a third of the third to will to go, a third of the third of the third to will to will to go. . . . I was only a few feet from the door and farther off than ever.

Miss Kay entered just then.

"Having trouble?"

I nodded that I was.

So Miss Kay took over: "Now, come on, what's the trouble?" She punctuated her question-without-the-inflection-of-a-question with a contraction of the arm that was cradling Meg's waist. It hit me with a jab in the small of my back. Hey, I felt that!

Meg's stance broke with the jab in the small of her back.

"Got the idea?" Miss Kay winked in my direction.

Got it. I understood what I saw well enough. Yes, Meg was ready to go for a walk now, for a walk away.

Although I hadn't intended to invite her, Miss Kay insisted on keeping us company. "In case you run into trouble again," she explained. We ignored her completely.

Meg watched the flow of concrete beneath her feet. I wanted to say something, something I really felt, for a change. Meg is my sister, after all, my only close kin, and she hadn't been well enough to bring home for twelve years. So something ought to have been said. Not the bland formula how-nice-to-have-you-home. But anything else was too sudden, too near. So I let the words by. And found myself saying, "It *is* a nice day, isn't it?"

22

Saturday was really beautiful, glossy with picture postcard colors. We went out for a picnic in the park, Meg and I. Meg met my eyes for the first time and smiled.

We have an unspoken agreement. If Meg's happy, I'm happy; if Meg smiles, I smile.

We strolled, dawdled our bare feet in the lake, lunched on a bench, walked some more. Then Meg gave me a chase, laughing all the while. I gave her a long lead, nine feet or ten. She veered off into a playground and I caught up with her there. She had saddled herself on the end of a seesaw and was peering up at me expectantly with the wide eyes of a child. In perfect understanding, I molded her fingers around the hand support. I saddled myself on the opposite end to counterbalance her. She is so light, I felt as if I were playing a dangerous game on a loose diving board. Our motion was abrupt, choppy. We rose and fell, rose and fell, now Meg, now myself ascendant.

People stared, I suppose, maybe even the children stared, but we couldn't be bothered.

She threw back her head, a hectic flush in her cheeks, her eyes gleaming. The wind loosened her hair, her long dark hair went flying. I took her off, prying her stiff hands loose. She clung to the board, then to me. The wind was up. Her hair whipped around her, across her eyes, against, between our lips, the heavy coiling hair of the drowned. It was as if something thought we might, didn't want us to, kiss.

Dr. Grey was back from vacation. We spent an hour with him. Before we left, he took me aside to offer a word of caution: "After all, you must remember that Meg may simply be reflecting your own feelings."

This was the cue for endless reassessment of my perceptions. Had Meg really been happy? Did she really smile? Her smile might have been anxiety—really the opposite of what it seemed. On the other hand, things are sometimes what they seem. Maybe she did smile, maybe she *was* happy. The question is: Which is the false theater, which the true? I'm not one to believe that all of a woman's sweetness is stifled violence. Some seemings are, they have to be. Or else?

Or else things are not what they seem. Children are built into the walls of buildings and the cornerstones of bridges to make them firm. I read that somewhere. Of course, the child is conned into it, tempted by the little grave, snug as a cubby, full of candy and toys. Could you prove this wasn't the case without razing all the bridges and buildings to the ground?

You couldn't be sure. In the meantime, it was best to take nothing for granted.

24

That evening Meg sat in the green armchair, the lamplight flaking round her shoulders. On her lap I placed the latest copy of *Life* magazine, open. On the page facing the story of interest was a luscious lobster dinner, a mayonnaise advertisement, complete with potato salad and pickle. Meg stared at the ad with some fixity, pursing her lips and raising the page closer to her eyes. Then she began to help herself, diving into the salad, tearing it to bits and stuffing her mouth with it. Clacking, chewing, coughing and spitting followed. I forced my hand into her mouth and cleared it, then ripped the magazine from her hands.

After the magazine was gone, she sat staring into her open hands. The magazine must have left an after-image, for she kept her hands in the same position, palms up, reading from left to right across them.

When she tired of that, she dropped her head and seemed to drowse. All you could see was a cascade of gilded hair falling onto a neck from some sort of promontory above it. I quickly tired of brushing her hair out of her face. Only once she lifted her face to look me in the eyes.

"How do you feel, Meg?" I asked, for the sake of saying something. I scarcely expected an answer.

"I feel with my fingers. Why? How do *you* feel?"

Then she added in a voice that was clear, incisive, sure: "You're insane—that goes without saying."

●

When I ventured out to the lavatory around eleven, I found Mr. Pinski wandering the corridor in a sort of trance, head down, and to all appearances listening to his feet. He's a fixture in the library: desk 42A. That desk is as much his as if he owned it. One of the elevator operators who's been here for twenty years says Mr. Pinski has been coming in regularly, nine sharp every morning, for as far back as he can remember. Nearly everyone knows him by name.

"Good morning, Mr. Pinski."

"What's that? Oh . . . to you, too. What's good about it?"

"The sun's shining. Wouldn't you agree that's good? How are you feeling today?"

"Not so good." His voice seemed very thick, not lately used, as if coming through wax.

"Sorry to hear that."

"What can you expect? An *alter trombenik* . . . old feller like me." He looked up: one peerless blue eye, one smoky eye. "Cataract," he explained, meaning the dusky eye.

"How's your research coming?"

26

"How does it look? I can't even find my desk; that's my first item of research—where to find my desk. Somebody else might be sitting there by mistake, what do you think? I've gone back three times, I don't see clearly. Help me, would you be so good?"

I offered my arm and we made our way slowly back to the reading room. I still couldn't muster up the courage to ask him exactly what the subject of his research was; today, clearly, wasn't the day. He has the reputation of having read one of the larger encyclopedias from first volume to last.

We came to his desk; I halted abruptly; he was about to walk on past.

"Here we are—42A," I said, pulling him back. Without question, the desk was his: his brown felt hat under the lamp, the worn gabardine jacket matching his trousers on the back of the chair, a book of word origins on the desk, a long legal pad beside it. "Look, isn't this yours?"

He stared at the desk as if he had never seen it before in his life. "Yes?" he asked, shaking his head. "Are you sure this is it?"

"Isn't this your jacket?"

"Could be . . . yes?" He held it at arm's length; he didn't put it on. He was still shaking his head, sadly or reproachfully, I couldn't tell which. "Never enough . . . What a time I had! *Mellech sobyetskis yoren*," he murmured. "It's been a feast. So it's over now?" Scouring my face for an answer.

27

"Over? What's over?"

"Time's up. Where did it all go? There's so much to know, never enough time. I hoped to live so long I'd be carried around in a basket. Today . . . I'm not well, it doesn't seem worth it."

Still shaking his head, he began to gather up his things.

"Are you really going? So soon?"

"How soon is soon? I've had a long life, a happy life. Youth is wonderful; treasure it. Time is precious, don't waste a minute of it."

He shook my hand solemnly. "Remember what I'm telling you."

I couldn't think of a word to say in reply. I shadowed him to the reading-room door. He tipped his hat to Tony, the security guard.

"*Nit heint, nit morgen . . .*" His words trailed after him.

"What's that he said?" asked Tony.

"I think he's leaving for good." The thought just then dawned on me.

"Not like Al Pinski, he just came. It isn't near lunchtime. That guy puts in an eight-hour day. I time myself by him, so I know. He's better than Bulova. Whatsa matter with him—he sick?"

"How should I know? I wouldn't count on his coming back if I were you."

"God," he muttered, "what a dump! This place is

a warehouse, cold storage. No action, nothing moves. It's dead. Unreal."

●

Saturday, I took Meg out shopping for some fall clothing. I'll never do it again. She froze into immobility at the first counter, gloves, and it was all I could do to move her far enough out of the thoroughfare to prevent a traffic jam. Yet she had embarked on the outing with big steps and all smiles.

With effort, I managed to park her in front of a manikin advertising the back-to-college look, plaid blazer, knee socks, a few cunning books of matching green and blue. I trusted Meg not to move. As quickly as possible I completed my errands. Without Meg's consent, I presumed to choose for her. Skirt, blouse, slip. I hate to buy women's clothing. I countered my embarrassment by explaining that these things were for my wife. Not that anyone cared.

When I was done, I found Meg still standing where I had placed her, by the entrance where the baby carriages were parked. She was imitating the manikin she faced, one arm bent at the elbow, the hand raised jauntily, the hip slung forward, the head at a rakish upward tilt, an exact mimicry, as if the manikin were

29

her mirror image. In this superficial fashion, aping the alien gestures without a clue as to what they signify, Meg understudies the human condition.

The crowd surged. From that heaving tide of shoppers, browsers, lifters, a small tot cut adrift. He reached out and clutched at Meg's skirt, then groped for the skirt of the manikin; the child was lost, blinded with tears; the manikin and Meg were both equally real or unreal to him. Meg tittered. A few shoppers paused to stare. At a mature woman, a woman no longer young, without errand, with nothing to do, a tennis ball in one hand, in the other the hand of someone else's child . . . a woman who unsettled them all.

On the way back I saw Meg in my mind's eye, dressed in what I had chosen for her, accusing me: "You've made me into a dummy, your dummy!" But at the start Meg came along quietly enough. We managed three blocks without a hitch. On the fourth, she began to giggle. Without warning, she broke loose and dashed ahead, running over the curb, into the street. I was caught by the light. By the time I got across she was halfway down the next block, spitting out commands: "Right foot! Left foot! Hay foot! Straw foot! Hut! Hump! Hoo! Hore!" and stepping along in brisk accord. As I came near, the orders changed: "Sit stand stopstick— Muck time—one—one—one—" I harnessed her, arm about her waist, and led her back to the house.

She came along quietly.

30

In the afternoon, Miss Kay dressed Meg for the party. "Let me help you dress, Meg. It's time, it's time."

"Dress . . ."

"Don't cry, what are you crying for? It's your birthday, a happy time. Your beau is coming, you lucky girl. Aren't you happy? Why aren't you happy? Are you unhappy because you should be happy and you're not? Don't cry, honey, it muddies the eyes. Let's see— what dress are we going to wear to the party? Which will it be? You have so many, Meg. Will it be this pretty one, or this pretty one, or this pretty one? Or this pretty one? Gosh, Meg, what a problem—they're all pretty. So many pretty dresses. How about this pastel? Hm?"

Meg played store dummy, head at a rakish upward tilt, hip slung forward, one arm bent at the elbow, the hand raised jauntily.

"The pastel it'll be then. Now—watch this!" Miss Kay held the dress on high.

Meg looked. Her hair was still in curlers; she was wearing a flowered dress with a white schoolgirl collar.

"Pretty? I'd say so, wouldn't you? Now there's something pretty to look at. You're an attractive woman, Meg, if only you'd let yourself be. If you'd only make a teeny effort. You've got a good figure, you're lucky that way. I wish I had your figure myself. Maybe you don't deserve what you've got because you don't appreciate it. Nobody deserves what they're born with, it's like having money in the bank without having to earn it. The least you can do is make good use of it. Think about that sometimes. Me—if I could take six inches off my you-know-where, my whole life would be different. I'd be swimming in luxury, you bet, I wouldn't have to lift a finger.

"How about some lipstick and rouge?—nothing flashy, just a touch—since it's your birthday, something special, and we're having a party.

"Now open your mouth, stretch your lips . . . Thata girl! I like this color, don't you? What's it called, I wonder? Honeyblush, that's a nice name, don't you think? Not too bold a color—refined—a nice touch. Now close your mouth, Meg. You don't look at all pretty with your mouth stretched open like that, in fact, you look like a fish. I only asked you to open your mouth to help the lipstick on. No, I don't think that's very funny. Close it at once, Meg! You're acting just like a baby. I know everyone's born with their mouths open, expecting candy, I suppose, and thinking they have a right to it because they expect it. Me, too, I'm only human. Stop kissing the mirror, Meg, I'll have to wash the glass. More work for me. You never think of it since you never work.

"All right, I'm giving you ten seconds to close your mouth. One, two, three . . . It'll freeze that way if

you don't stop it. How'd you like to go around with a
puss like that for the rest of your life, hm? . . . Nine,
ten, that's enough. That does it! I'm going to force
your jaw shut unless you shut it yourself this instant—
I'm warning you, it'll hurt.

"Help! Ooo—damn—"

It was Miss Kay, not Meg, hurting.

"Was that a nice thing to do? Is it nice to bite me—
even just a nip? Even in fun? I don't think it's nice,
I don't think it's at all funny, and I don't think it's
funny kissing me now, Meg, you don't mean it, you
faker, not a bit you don't. Okay, I like you too. Sometimes. Hey, that tickles! Hah, hah . . . No, I'm not
laughing because it's funny but because I'm ticklish.
Cut that out, Meg! Or I'm going to quit right now!
Do you hear me? Stop licking me. This minute! You're
not a cat.

"How many years old, and that's the way you be-
have. You're over thirty, Meg. Some grown-up lady!"

Meg hung her head.

"All right, all right, I forgive you. I can see you're
sorry, all right, I hope you mean it. What gets into
you? Gremlins? Let's give your hair ten extra brushes
till it shines and forget all about it, whadya say? Okay?
Tell me anything you want, anything you think of. A
penny for your thoughts, Meg. Talk, Meg, talk to me,
it makes the work go easier."

Meg considered for a moment, then said, "Kindness
itself." Tenderly.

"That's a very nice thing to say, Meg. You can be very nice when you try, you ought to try more often."

Then Meg said, "Dark work, dark work."

"Now, *that* isn't very nice. That's hooey. It doesn't make any sense. How can work be dark? It can be heavy, heavy or light, mine is heavy sometimes, like now, when you don't help me out. Whenever you say something nice, you cancel it out by saying something that doesn't make sense or sounds mean the very next thing. The way you said that sounded mean. You're not really mean, I'm sure you're not. Why do you say mean-sounding things then?"

Meg's head was down.

"Now then, now then, aren't we something to look at?"

"Look at," said Meg. "We are something."

"You—I mean you. You're quite a glamour girl. Didn't I fix you up nice? We ought to have a camera."

Meg studied the mirror.

"Isn't that a nice dress?"

"A nice dress," said Meg.

"For your birthday."

"For your birthday."

"No, Meg, *your* birthday. And your hair shines."

Meg looked down at her feet.

"Shoes—we've forgotten your shoes, Meg. How could we forget a thing like that?

"There we go. All ready now. Take a good look before we go, Meg. Isn't that a pretty sight? Gosh, I look a mess. Now we'll settle you in the living room while I get dressed. It won't be long. I wonder where your brother disappeared to, all of a sudden. Funny— he was just here a minute ago. Hiding? Taking a peek at the goodies, I bet. There you go. It's my turn now, I'd better pretty myself up."

In the evening, the birthday party for Meg. I forget which birthday it was. A few years ago I stopped counting, for both of us. Tim showed up as he has every year, although their engagement has been off for more than ten years. Last year, and the years before, we gathered at the hospital. I've often wondered about Tim, why it is that he has never married. It would be perfectly understandable after all these years. He really should consider himself free. But he shows up again as if no years have intervened. We're an alumni association perpetuating—I don't know what.

Poor devoted Tim! Visiting his apartment, I'm always struck by some detail or other that points to the same sad fact: Tim lives like a man in a condemned building, like an uninvited guest at his own feast. Is it Meg who's done this to him?

Once I dropped my keys under his bed and happened to take a long look under it. Shoes, nothing odd in that—but all apparently singles. A full fleet of mismatched shoes, looking charred, useless, dusty as beached boats. How could anyone manage to lose single shoes when shoes always come and go in pairs?

Last visit, it was the paper plates that struck me. We had turned on the light in the kitchen to make some coffee. There were three paper plates on the table, one in front of each chair, a big serving spoon in each, a mug with a milk rim, a carton of milk gone warm and sour. At first I thought he might have had guests, but the big spoons and the remnants of meat sauce, hardened to glue on the tablecloth, spoke of solitary manners.

"Breakfast," he explained, pointing to one plate. "Lunch," to another. "Supper—over there—Irma!— Jane!—Francesca!" He chuckled and began to clear the table, throwing the spoons into the sink, the stale milk down the drain, and tossing the paper plates into the open dumbwaiter.

"I ought to marry, really. The roaches are getting out of hand," he said in startling juxtaposition. "Sometimes I eat out of the bag I buy my groceries in— that's not a way to live. You know what I mean?"

Tim brought a gift to the party, as he has every year. Even Dr. Grey put in an appearance before it was all over.

Tim's present was a woolen scarf, wine-colored. It was really a man's scarf, but it's the thought that counts. Meg received it blindly. I watched her closely. Her eyes, the irises, were wheels spinning in sand. She turned the irises up into her lids: her eyes were white, the white eyes of Lot's wife, mirroring forever the salt plain. Taking the scarf up in her right hand, she lifted it high above her head, waving it slowly to and fro, a trophy of something. Of what contest? Survival? Was that all?

Miss Kay's present was a year's subscription and first copy of *Time* magazine. She winked unsubtly (you could hear the shutter clicking) and said, looking in my direction, "That way *neither* of you gets bored."

This time her sarcasm was unmistakable.

My contribution was of another ilk entirely. It came boxed but not wrapped. A piebald kitten, white, with a black ear and one black paw. Miss Kay and Tim exchanged veiled glances when I presented the kitten to Meg. But Meg's smile made it all worthwhile, despite their mockery. I had wanted to give Meg something alive, something all her own, more her own than the children she'll not now ever have.

"What do you think you'll call him?" I pressed Meg.

She considered a moment. Then answered softly, "You."

I was touched, deeply touched.

"Well, you've got all the time in the world," Miss Kay put in. "There's no hurry in fixing a name. You'll have to have him spayed or fixed or whatever they call it—" All this directed at me, not Meg. "And if you want any furniture left, you'll have to have his claws removed. An awful nuisance if you ask me."

But no one *had* asked her.

We settled ourselves in the dining room. Miss Kay brought in ice cream, cake, and grape soda in waxed cups, as if it were some child's sixth or seventh birthday. She hitched up her harlequin glasses, then began singing "Happy Birthday to You." Meg surprised us by joining in, giggling as she did so. It took me a moment to recall that "You" was the kitten. And so we were all singing happy birthday to him. The key set by Miss Kay was too high for me and my voice emerged falsetto, cracked. Tim emitted some shapeless, grumbling sounds. His face was red with embarrassment or effort, and his eyes cast down. I noticed his baldness for the first time.

Just as we started to cut the cake, Dr. Grey joined us. He helped himself to a wedge, and then another. He ate with gusto, a way of covering his lack of anything to say. Taken altogether, it was what kids really think of summer camp: a long unplanned party where nobody has any fun. The sweets spoiled our appetites for supper.

Before leaving, Tim kissed Meg goodbye: three times lightly on the left cheek. As if blotting a delicate word like "stiletto."

The effort at gaiety had exhausted us all. Meg fell into actual or sham sleep after five-thirty, and there was nothing I could do to rouse her.

Feeding the kitten, letting him out and in, will have to be my responsibility. That is, to begin with. I have large hopes. For the present, I hope that the kitten will take to Meg's lap. If nothing else, Meg is a good lap.

●

Lately I've been noticing a contraction of Meg's left hand, the fingers clenched so tightly that they leave red holes in the palm. I'm going to try massaging the hand each morning, fifteen minutes at a time. This means I'll have to get up before seven. I'm also going to see whether a rubber ball, wedged between fingers and palm and kept there as long as possible, will help to break the stiffness. I expect—the first time—it will feel like forcing a bud.

Monday, when the alarm rang, I woke with one word on my lips.
"Ratcatcher!"
That's how it was and always is on Monday.
I wake up with my fingers welded to my palms, my fingers stiff as bullets, my knuckles white, my hands—fists.
On my way to work, I keep bumping into people. Really, I get a bang out of obstructing people, de-

railing the invisible tracks on which they run. Whenever this happens, instead of saying "So sorry," I say "How are you?" Sometimes my victim is so harried, so baffled and unsure, that he follows up by asking after my health as well. But more often he stares at me as if I've just said something obscene, as if it weren't enough that I stepped on his toe, but I have to insult him to boot.

This Monday, the man I detained for a minute was so angry, so eager to be angry, that he hallooed the cop on the corner.

"Like I said, officer, this here guy's the one. He accosted me. There's a law, isn't there a law?"

"Accosted you? Do you know what 'accosted' means?" My voice rose. Illiteracy, belligerency, and no chin besides, all this fuss a diversionary cloud round his chinlessness.

"All right, boys, break it up. What's up? What's the charge? I don't have all day. Who started it?"

"I was greeting him, that's all. Trying to be nice."

"Greeting . . . there's no law against greeting somebody. Weren't soliciting, were you? Just friendly greetings? You're buddies, then?"

"Huh? Never laid eyes on him in my life. That's a fact."

"Do you know this man, Mr—?"

"Henken, Richard Henken. There—I give my name freely, I've nothing to hide. Not personally. I don't know him that way—"

"In *no* way," put in the chinless wonder.

"But he's a fellow creature and so I thought—"

"Fellow creature? Did you hear that? You slob. Am I an animal? Did you hear him call me an animal, officer? The nerve, the nerve of some people! Being as you're no better than a mutt yourself, Hank!"

The policeman spread his blue arms wide as a pope's blessing between us. "All right, boys, no charge. Break it up before it's too late. I'll book you both next time. It takes two to tango. Break it up, keep moving. What's this?"

A small crowd was gathering.

"There's nothing to see, folks. Nobody's disturbing the peace. Somebody got up on the wrong side of the bed this morning, that's all. Keep moving . . . that's it. Keep moving along. . . . Who likes to go to work in the morning? Do I? Do you think I like to? Does anyone? Do you have to make a fuss about it? What are you people waiting for? Whatsa matter—you *want* trouble? If you're so hard up for excitement, go to the movies, join the force, try my beat at two in the morning. I can't book a man for being a wise guy, can I? Okay, Mr. Hemp, there's only one way to break this up. You started this monkey business, you end it. Scram! I'll count six. And watch your step. There'd better not be a next time."

He was playing to the crowd now.

"Next time, I won't let you off so easy."

It was all beneath notice. I moved on, breaking my

way loose from the small crowd which had formed, gapers and gawkers, faces with slots for eyeholes.

What if I were to hold up a man on the street—at gunpoint, say—until I got an answer to my question: "How are you? Are you?" I've asked this question in all kinds of ways, softly, loudly, imperiously, entreatingly, but I've never, ever, gotten an answer. If I really stood my ground and insisted on an answer, no doubt the police would come first. There'd be an angry crowd. I'd never get to know.

It was all beneath notice. I walked on. The fact is: I *was* arrested once, a couple of years ago, on a morals charge. I was sitting with three strangers, two men and a woman, at a cafeteria table, trying to get them to hold hands so the current of love might pass through us from one to another. Naturally it was a flop. They didn't even love themselves, so there was no love to spare.

There was no one else in the office when I arrived. The ritual greetings and solicitations were yet to come. A library early in the morning before the readers arrive is a peaceful place, a graveyard. Only the janitor, Gabriel, was up and about, mopping and humming to himself. He's always humming, even when you don't hear him, he's humming subvocally and if you wait around long enough it's sure to surface: hymn bursts, advertising jingles, chants, hit tunes, election slogans, rounds. This morning it was all about Delia.

"Tony shot B'Delia
'Twas on a Friday night.
First time he shot her
She bowed her head
An' died.
Delia's gone, gone,
Delia's gone,
One more round . . .
Delia's gone, gone,
Delia's gone. . . ."

Each round brought on a broad swathe of the mop.
He might equally well have been singing

Cast out, expunge,
Expunge. . . .

Susan was the first to arrive. "You're looking cheerful," she said. "How *can* you at this time of the day and week?"

"Operation bootstrap," said I, "moral facelift."

"Well, I'm here!" It was Pete. "And considering the magnitude of that achievement, I think I'll rest on my laurels the rest of the day."

"Shit," said Arragan-Horgan.

"They ought to declare Monday a permanent disaster area," suggested Simon.

"Hello, everyone," said Mr. MacFinster. "Another week's upon us. Another day, another dollar."

43

We said the same thing, with minor variations, every Monday morning.

When Nathan Haglim worked with us, he had two phrases to cover all bad times: "It'll pass" and "You get used to it." It always passed, but as to whether he got used to it, no one knows. He disappeared without a trace one day about a year ago. He didn't ask to have references forwarded. He didn't even bother to resign.

The litany wasn't over yet. On my way out to the public catalog, Mary turned to me. "What are you looking so happy about? Haven't you heard? It's Monday morning. And as if that isn't bad enough, we're about to be visited."

The others joined in chorus: "When? When?"

"No one knows when," MacFinster reminded us, giving us the cue to disperse and to settle down to business. "No one knows when—that's the whole point."

Under our breaths, we whispered about the arrival of the great efficiency expert, magnifying his greatness. "Are you ready? Are you ready?" was the question of the hour.

I had a hunch we'd be waiting for quite a few months before anyone did descend upon us.

On to wash my glasses, then on to the pencil sharpener, then to the laying out of tools: number 3-H hard pencils, number 2 soft pencil, pen, pad, eraser, Exacto knife, ruler, dust cloth, paper clips at the ready,

44

rubber bands—anything else? I am poised, on the brink of, able to— The preliminaries are, alas, over.

MacFinster called me into his office later in the morning.

"Are you challenged by your job, Mr. Henken? Does it test your mettle?"

"To the very limit," I replied with all my heart. "Sometimes it's almost more than I can handle. My desk—"

"Good, good, I'm glad to hear it." MacFinster comforted his hands, one conferred a little pat of encouragement on the other. "You won't be bored then. The man who was there before you—"

"You mean Ernest Coke?"

"Yes, Mr. Coke—how did you know? Word travels, I suppose. Mr. Coke just seemed to drift off at the end. Don't know why, he was fine to start with. One day I found him sitting at his desk and dealing out a deck of cards. They were catalog cards and he was playing a game of solitaire—as nearly as I could make out. Most unfortunate. A pity, really. I sometimes think that desk of yours is placed too far away from fresh air. I'm a great believer in fresh air. But we have a space problem, you know. Only look around. We're packed like sardines, I know. It's too bad, but that's the way matters stand, a tight budget, funds cut, and so on. So we all suffer. We *all* suffer, Richard, believe me, myself included. I hope you don't mind my calling you Richard. I understand your problem, you don't have to tell me about it, but we're all cramped, and your desk has to stay where it is. Sorry, but that's the way the cookie crumbles, that's how it is, one of the small sacrifices exacted from each of us for the common good." MacFinster punctuated the air, forefinger on high. "What's best for all of us is best for each of us," he concluded. Then, making sure he had left nothing out:

"And visa versa," he added.

"More particularly vice versa," I thought aloud.

"Come again? How's that?"

"I said I'll bear with the desk I have until there's a chance for another."

"Something to bear in mind, Mr. Henken—something I used to tell Mr. Coke. Keep asking yourself, Is it the desk that makes the man, or the man that makes the desk? Something to think about."

"I'll remember that."

"Fine. That's the spirit."

All in all, a rough Monday. I looked forward to a quiet evening. But when I arrived home, the minute I opened the door, it was kiss of gas. Gas all over the house.

I went straight to the kitchen and opened the window. The wall of the room seemed to be swooning in a thick yellow vapor, although the dials of the stove were all off. The pilot light was on and steady: I checked. Someone must have righted the knobs a few minutes before I opened the door. But who?

Meg was asleep in the easy chair. Miss Kay was nowhere to be seen. I was very annoyed—and with reason. I've told Miss Kay time and time again never to leave Meg alone. How could she have forgotten? Or had she thought the little minute it took to fetch the mail not worth counting?

I would have to speak to her. Firmly.

What followed was an ugly scene. Recriminations, too sordid, too humdrum really, to repeat. Afterward I overheard Miss Kay on the phone. She must have been seeking advice from Dr. Grey because I heard the phrases "trying to be supportive" and double mention of "elevators"—was it elevators? Dr. Grey must have counseled patience, because she answered, "All right, I'll give it time . . . a few weeks more . . . if I can bear it."

●

Saturday we took the bus out to Plum Beach. Meg was no more conspicuous in her immobility than any other determined sunbather. Except for the fact that it was the end of the summer and the pallor of her skin was striking, so white as to be almost blue. And her feet looked strange, the toenails too long, curled under, stony as horns. I would have to remember to trim them.

"Well," said Miss Kay, "I suppose you think that's pretty funny. Spreading out an extra towel for her Ladyship, dirtying a perfectly clean towel because she's too special to sit on the blanket with the rest of us."

"It's because—"

"Don't tell me, I don't want to hear. Always special treatment, always a special reason for the special treatment. Your sister is spoiled, spoiled rotten. Sometimes I think it's as simple as that. Sometimes I think it's all an act she's putting on so as to get her own way. I know that's not what the textbooks say, I've read all that about its being a sickness and all and how she can't help acting the way she does, but that's not the way it feels to me right now. Look at us—she's got us where she wants us, hasn't she, waiting on her hand and foot. Never worked a day in her life, I bet, never roughed up her satiny smooth hands. Thinks herself a duchess, and no wonder."

The glare, Miss Kay's monotone, filled me with sleep. I stayed behind my twin lids, a heavy golden penny on each; if I moved, they would tumble.

48

"Now, see here! You handle this."

Miss Kay was shaking me. In the little time I wasn't paying attention, Meg had managed to turn herself over and had half-buried herself in the sand. It was her face that worried me. She was nose deep in it, pouring it over her hair, her ears.

"Please don't—please," I coaxed. "I'll bury the rest of you in the sand if you like the feel of it. But you'll have to turn over. And not your head. You might suffocate. Besides, if I'm going to bury you, I'd like you to appreciate it!" I giggled as I cajoled her, a shallow, flat, mirthless accompaniment, more tic than laugh.

She went limp as a rag doll. I rolled her body over and began to pour sand over her trunk, arms, legs. She lay there unresisting, eyes closed, smiling.

"Here's salt and pepper, rice and raisins. . . . Pay attention, Meg."

"Count me out of this discussion," said Miss Kay.

"I'm stitching you a magic quilt of spools and sprockets, burrs and buttons, bells and prisms. . . . Look out, Meg! I am raining nibbles . . ." I rambled on playfully.

"Good Lord, one as fruity as the other," muttered Miss Kay to the picnic basket.

But, of course, I knew very well what I was handling. Sand . . . ruins of mountains, cliffs, boulders, bones. Sand . . . glint of perhaps diamond chafing glass. I sifted a cupful from hand to hand, the grains quieting in a heap shaped by the funnel of my palm. So the most enduring are ground down. . . .

Back at home, we bathed Meg. I had to scoop up whole handfuls of sand from the drain before the water would go down. It seemed as if Meg herself were crumbling to grains, breaking up particle by particle, marzipan lady—not quite soluble, so caked with sand.

Sunday morning, I heard a scuffling at my door, a whine. It was You, tail down, mincing with fear. Miss Kay had just booted her off the sofa.

●

Right foot down, left foot down. On my way to work I make up stories. They make the time pass and keep me from asking impertinent questions. My stories never go far, but they do get me to the library steps. Once upon a time . . . the incantation begins. And before I know it, on the wave of an invisible wand, I'm at the double doors.

Once upon a time there was a man named Smith who wanted to write stories. He was very good at first lines. In no time at all, he had heaps of beginnings.

—On the night of the blackout, Liz and Mike made love but not to each other.

—I am living at the bottom of a well. It is really very comfortable here and I see no point in moving.

—One afternoon, after inserting a dime and a nickel in the coffee machine according to instructions, Fred found that nothing happened. Bent coin? He pressed the return-change lever: nothing. He pounded on the machine with his fist. That did it; he heard his money being swallowed. There was a hum, then the click that preceded the descent of the cup. Only this time, instead of the cup, a tiny man appeared in a plumber's coverall. He was not quite three inches high. "I am the master of the machine," he said. "What is your desire?"

—In the chill bleak hours between midnight and dawn, Joseph Audsley was preparing a nightcap to cap his preceding nightcap. "Whiskey weather," he muttered, "brrrr—" Then he heard a muffled commotion in the hall, the elevator door opened, and he could hear the wheels of a wagon scraping through the corridor—no footsteps. Hm . . . Joseph stood pressed against his door, three bolts drawn, and opened the viewing slot. All he could see through it was the viewing slot of the door across from his, and then, in the center of the slot, a bubble: the eye of his neighbor, also watching. . . .

—Once upon a time, in the time beyond all time, when all you had to do to fall asleep was to take off your hat, there lived a sultana who did not sleep. Now some said she could not sleep, while others said she would not sleep, some others said she would not sleep because she could not sleep, while still others said she could not sleep because she would not sleep. I leave it to you why she did not sleep; all I can say is—she did not sleep. And this was strange since it was so easy to fall asleep. What could be easier than taking off your hat?

Not unpromising beginnings. But because Smith was a busy man, a cloth merchant, and because he was something of a scatterbrain, his stories never got beyond the larval stages.

He wrote out these beginnings on the backs of coupons, bills of sale, remittances, ticket stubs, and inter-office memos, and he stuffed them all into the pocket of his overcoat. He had a feeling that any one of them might hatch at any moment, and so he didn't dare leave them at the office, but took them everywhere he went.

Then, one noon, on his way back from lunch, crossing the street and mulling over his latest beginning, he walked into a moving bus. He never recovered. His papers fell out. The wind whipped up and shuffled and scattered his beginnings all over the street. A dog peed on one. A bird put another in her nest. A man working in a manhole wrapped up the remains of his lunch in a third—

So it goes. . . . My story goes nowhere, but I've arrived. My destination. I face the double doors of the library. The mural in the entrance hall shows some great goddess figure of Enlightenment in sandals and helmet; she is stout and toga-clad, built like a Greek wrestler. A massive sword idles on her lap, useless. She holds a lamp aloft; its rays dart out. Beneath the lamp is an oily, writhing mass of dragons and snakes: Greed, Superstition, and Ignorance, the color of bilge water, darkly gleaming. They are trying to escape from the burning arrows of the lamp and are getting badly twisted up in each other instead. The inscription reads: *Animis Opibusque Parati.* Arragan-Horgan claims to have seen the inscription change at regular intervals like the names on a movie marquee, inscriptions ranging from *Ad Astra Per Aspera, Dum Spiro, Spero,* to *Aut Veniam Viam, Aut Feciam.* And once: *Kumquats Anyone?*

At work, during a dull moment, Sandy asked idly, "Do you believe in ghosts?"

"No—I don't believe in ghosts, auras, astral projection, divination through yarrow stalks, or ESP," I answered at once, the soul of sensibleness. What a question! I didn't explain that I lived with ghosts nearly all of the time. And who doesn't? Not the ghosts of the dead—there are those, too—but the ghosts of the living, the ghosts of today, the "I saids," "You saids," "He saids," crowding me out, making noise, bubbling and hissing like acids, like gas. I'm never alone; they never leave me alone.

After two weeks of mulling over the options, I offered You to Anne, the new secretary. She's been looking for a household pet. "Something small and clean," I overheard her saying. "How about a shrew?" suggested Mary, "I've seen some that could fit in a thimble."

I offered to throw in five pounds of kitty litter plus a two-week supply of dry and canned cat food, and, as if these free additions were the deciding factor, Anne accepted the cat. So much for my experiment with household pets. It's been too much trouble. The kitten is simply not made for laps, as the cat, unbeautiful, fat and old, may well be. The sad part is, I don't think that Meg will miss the kitten at all. I'm not sure that she'll even notice that he's gone. Whenever I placed You on Meg's lap, she made no motion to receive the kitten, and whenever I left Meg alone, she lifted the poor thing by the tail, suspending him from as high as her arm could stretch. Add to all this the fact that, as far as I'm concerned, even a kitten's most kittenish capers are boring, and the conclusion is foregone: You must go.

●

The psychiatrist as fortune cookie. Dr. Grey says:

Be cautious, yet confidently aggressive. ● Many changes of mind and mood. Do not hesitate too long. ● Proceed with caution. ● You are a courageous person. ● Pass for now, the risk is too great. ● Your efforts will result in much profit. ● Proceed with caution. ● Sometimes the best gain is to lose. ● A pleasant experience, do not pass it by. ● Give what you have to someone. It may be better than you think. ● Proceed with caution. ● You will have to choose between two jobs.

This last is fortune number 6678934 and I am weary of plucking such straws.

●

What staggers me is not the persistence of illusion, but the persistence of the world in the face of illusion.

There is really nothing wrong with Meg's muscles except for the atrophy of long disuse. It's as if she simply let knife and fork drop one day, saying, "I don't care." And the estrangement was final, binding. Could it be as simple and as fatal as this, "I don't care"?

Meg is a poet who has never written a line, a painter who has never put a stroke to canvas, hence, the

55

perfect artist. The trouble with Meg is that she has a kind of integrity, a strange integrity, it is true, the integrity of a vacuum chamber. In order for her to get well, she'd have to be shattered, and the world would rush in with conditions and demands, real flesh on the knife. It would be a crime, a crime that begs to be committed.

Today we embarked on a long walk: I figured on crossing the park at the very least, but we ended up not a block from home, bench-squatting on the traffic island in the middle of Eighty-sixth Street and Broadway. It turned out to be a good long sit, a couple of hours. The sun was up, the wind cold, the sun bright as a blade, the air corrosive. Only a few of the old folks were out. A woman, who did not know how it stood with us, tried to engage Meg in conversation. Meg did not respond. She was absorbed in studying her hands: they lay flat in her lap, a fan of ten bones. The old woman muttered bitterly, "A word to the lonely—sunshine to the sad. It can't be bought."

I tried to say something mollifying, but the old woman answered with a snap of her purse. When I explained that I was only trying to be friendly, she said, "I wasn't talking to *you*, so don't interfere. I don't talk to men. I'm not *that* kind."

It wasn't long before she tottered off.

Meg stared at the sun, then at her feet. After about an hour of this, she turned to me and said, "It's a garden." What was? I tried to see what she saw.

Although not everyone would think it at first glance, it was a garden of sorts we were sitting in. True, it wasn't much of a garden—concrete mostly, with a few stiff weeds gouging their way between the cracks. There was a lattice, but it lay flat along the ground in the concrete, and there were no roses trailing across it. Staring hard at the sun, Meg supplied the roses, red, yellow, then bruise-colored. Sun stains, actually, retinal sizzle. In point of fact, the lattice—grid, to be exact—lay over the subway tracks and was an escape hatch for fumes. I knew this; did Meg know it too?

It grew rapidly colder. An old man scattered crumbs on the ground for the birds. The pigeons jabbered and poked between Meg's shoes, as if between stones.

Sunday morning Meg slept late. Why she observes the workingman's Sabbath is something I can't fathom; after all, every morning is Sabbath for Meg. I read the newspaper made fat for my Sunday boredom. Haven't times changed? Yes. For the better? Yes. It is now possible to dial a number in the morning and fly to the Bahamas in the afternoon, to come in singles, triples, pairs. Walk right up and say Hi! Swimming in the morning, jai alai, golfing, rolfing in the afternoon. Think of it: rolfing! That means no more groping, tongue-biting, leg-crossing, stammering, hesitation, but presto plunge: pull the plug and out come rushing—instant intimacy! With anyone! Intimacy guaranteed or your money back. Come one, come all. From Oskaloosa come, from Rawalpindi, from Athens, Georgia—come! Walk right up and say, Hi there! Now, gals, it is possible to have a screen test topless (confidence respected), while your companion of the day or week or hour orders his gin tonic, anchovies, and toast. For mature people only. Two-fisted joy! O arc! Swift transit! Go quickly—whee! Go friendly—gee!

Today is Sunday, October seventh, the two hundred and eightieth day of the year with eighty-five more days to follow. The moon is blue. The morning stars are Mars and Saturn. A year ago yesterday, some high government official said that the war was definitely winding down. On this day in history, Heinrich Melchior Mühlenberg, founder of the Lutheran Church of America, died in 1787. The first railroad in the United States was put into operation by the Granite Railroad Company of Massachusetts in 1826. In 1849, Edgar Allan Poe died in Baltimore, and the Hoosier poet James Whitcomb Riley was born in Indiana.

And what do you think is happening today? Nothing. Simply nothing. Meg refuses to acknowledge the day; she won't stir from the bed. Every hour I make a visit to her bedside with some bright comment, with the dull question of whether she needs.

So the day passed and it was night.

In the middle of the night, I woke slowly, my dream

invaded by a white cloud, a bright, cold presence. At the other end of the hall a light was on. She stood in the dim light, spectral in her white gown. I rose at once.

She whispered, "Now don't you tell anyone. You're insane. Meg doesn't walk on her own. You're just imagining things." She cupped her left breast in her right hand as if to weigh it, as if to magnify its weight. Then she closed the door softly. Slut! I stepped out into the hallway, which seemed to descend, I plunged after her, after her shadow, vaporizing down the corridor.

She was already in bed when I got to her, sheets unruffled over her still limbs. Lying in darkness, watching, listening, not asleep, but not what you would call awake.

I simply need more sleep myself.

●

I can hear very well from my desk. I'm not really that far from the center of activities in the room, but what with pillars and file cabinets strewn like thicket, gibbet, and hedge on all sides, I'm quite remote, in fact, I'm hardly ever visible. The roof of the cataloging room has always struck me as low, oppressively, even dangerously, low. The massive weight of the dead above, I suppose, a mountain of words pressing down upon us. Why else the innumerable columns—braces and splints—unless the ceiling is heavier than the walls alone can bear?

I was only yards away when he came in, but well stashed under a little tumulus of papers and pamphlets, deeply hidden in my corner. I heard the man announcing he had a gift to make to the library. I made a slow half-circle in my chair to size up my client: no visible prosperity. The mackintosh he was in the process of removing was several sizes too large. Under it, no better: a blue suit of some cheap fabric, shiny as paper.

"Gift to the library—monetary?" prompted Mary. There was a lilt in her voice, ascendant on the syllable "mon," sinking down rapidly on "tary."

"Afraid not. The other kind."

"Oh, you mean books, pamphlets, that kind of thing. Right over there—" A curt wave of her hand in my direction.

"Where?"

"Look—where I'm pointing. Do you see?"

"I don't quite."

I wanted to laugh. I could have announced my presence but preferred simply to sit and look on, silent and unhelpful. Would he discover me? Was I really there? I was waiting to find out.

"Now— Follow my hand. Are you following?"

"Oh, yeah, now I see."

In a few strides he was upon me.

"Hello?" I indicated the low stool alongside my desk. My visitors are few and these few not to be encouraged, so I don't have a full-fledged chair.

He smiled faintly, made a dusting motion with his fingertips, sat. Everything about him looked second-hand, borrowed, thumbed over, soiled; he was soiled to the yellow of his eyes. "Work-worn"—the phrase come to life.

"I don't believe we've met. My name is Valparosi, Nicholas Valparosi. You can call me Nick."

"Richard Henken. Pleased to meet you. What can I do to help you?"

He placed a large manila envelope on my desk. It was bulging, free-form, didn't look much like a book. It humped quietly between us.

"Are you waiting for me to do the honors? Please— you do, I insist." He urged the packet upon me.

Chicken in a basket for two?

"Oh, all right." I lifted the flap and dug in. I removed something which bore a striking resemblance to a jam jar. Jam jar it was. Label still intact: Marmalade.

But it appeared to be full of ash.

"There's more," he said. "Just a sec." He withdrew a sheaf of paper I hadn't noticed. It had a brown, curling edge.

"Well, all this is very mysterious."

"This is—was—my life work," he explained.

"That so? That's too bad."

"Yeah, sad."

"But what was it?"

"A book, would you believe it? I know I don't look the type that writes books, but that's what it was. Four hundred and twelve pages. Near eight years of my life. Every night pounding away, a tin piano—not much music in it. All I got left is this last page I'm holding in my hand."

"Sorry to hear it. But what can I do?"

"Wait and hear what I have to say."

"Much as I would like to listen," I explained, "my time is not my own."

"Do I hear a ghost note? Give some slack, brother. Where you going in such a hurry? What's five minutes of your life? Take five. A little patience, you'll live longer. Yessir, patience, let me tell you . . . I know." He leaned forward, lowering his voice. The rest would be for my ears alone.

"I've been a salesman all my life."

He paused, giving me time to take this in.

"I see."

"No, you *don't* see, I'm sure. You can't know what that means if you haven't been one yourself. And I don't mean bunions. All my life I've been a salesman. I earned an honest living, and I'm not proud of it. Thirty years . . . you name it, I sold it: toys, haberdashery, shoes—on my knees, hardware, Sani-Flush, bathroom fixtures, kitchen gadgets, gimmicks—Valparosi at your service. Junk, trash, rubbish, all of it a waste, one brand no better than the other. And what had any of them to do with me? *Me*, understand! My one and only life. A guy can lose his self-respect—he can lose his *self*—I know I almost did. I used to come home and break dishes, smash them up. That was an expensive habit, let me tell you, and me piss-poor. Then it dawned on me to write a book. When exactly it was, how the bug got me, I don't remember. Out of the blue, like. Anyhow, I made up my mind to write a book instead of busting up the house. Everybody was writing books: waiters, junkies, whores, so why not me? I figured even if it didn't hit the jackpot and roll me in money, at least it would give me a boost. It would give me a lift to see my name in print. And writing it would give me something to do, ease out the poisons maybe. So I got myself a typewriter and started battering away at it, one letter at a time. I didn't touch a dish except to eat off it. I was a changed man."

"And this is it?" I lifted the jam jar, tilted it to the light. An ill-digested fragment of shoestring sifted clear of the dust.

"Is—was. That book was my reason for going on. First my wife says I'm a violent man, then she says I'm not a man at all, but a clerk. To make the story short—she left me. Cleaned me out. Took the furniture, curtains, rugs, good dishes, was kind enough to leave me the kitchen table and chairs, a bed, a coffeepot and the Teflon frying pan. When I saw her next—it was April and we split up in February—she was already arm in arm with a buyer I knew from Gimbels. Me, I don't grudge her, she did well for herself. Live and let live, I say. I have no patience for women since that time. Waste of money, waste of energy, waste of time. Writing a book ate up all my time. And I'm not a writing man; it hurts me to write a letter even. I'm not even much of a reading man. So believe me, it wasn't easy to write a page, let alone a whole book. For every page I kept, I tore up more than I counted. Four hundred and twelve pages times, let's say, ten, that makes—how many pages did I write? You figure that out. And slaving from nine to five on top of it all."

"Well, we all have to work. Right now I'm pressed for time. What you're telling me is very interesting but right now I have all this dreary paper work in front of me, no more inspiring than Sani-Flush, I assure you. But I've got to get on with it. I've got to eat, my family has to eat. Fact of life." I caught myself sounding like someone I knew very well but couldn't place. And then I placed the echo: Mac-Finster.

"Gotcha! You're asking me to hurry again, to get on with it. Aren't you dying to know how my life work ended up in this bottle here?"

"If you want to talk about it. But briefly—"

"In a word: thugs. Hoodlums. Eight years of my life to a heap of ashes. Know how long it took? Minutes, two minutes flat. Two lousy minutes."

"I'm very sorry to hear that. But why didn't you keep a copy? Can't you reconstruct most of it, or part of it, from memory? Like start from the last page and work backward?"

"You kidding? You got to be kidding. Four hundred and twelve pages? Eight years? I'm older than when I started . . ." He sighed and opened his hands: empty.

"Mr. Valparosi, what can I do to help you?"

"I want you—the library—to have this."

"We can't keep the jar here. But I'll keep this last page in my file if you want—"

"Okay, and read it. Will you read it?"

"Not now. I'll read it, but I can't now. My boss—understand? I promise you, word of honor, I'll read it."

"So okay," he agreed reluctantly. "It's a deal, fair and square. Let's leave it at that."

"It's a promise, count on me. I'll read it." I put the jar in his hands.

"Can you find your way out? Should I show you the way?"

"Take it easy, mister, don't worry. I'm going. Bum's rush, eh? I can take a hint."

He stood up and began flailing around.

"Forgotten anything?"

"Hat."

"But you weren't wearing a hat when you came in."

"No, I never do. I'm leaving now." He did a little dance: shuffle, tap, the briefest of bows, then made straight for the door.

Ever onward. I faced my desk.

But I couldn't resist taking a peek at the page he had left face down on the blotter. I wouldn't read it, I would only just peek.

It took me no time at all to read it:

–412–

piteously said.

Then a yawning white space.

Then:

The end.

That was it. A small hoot escaped me. It subsided to a chuckle, followed by a little catch in the throat, a touch of what Arragan-Horgan calls "sediment." This was the last shard of something, some edifice raised with effort and pain; who knew how much effort

or how much pain or whether it stood for even a ram-
shackle moment? I didn't even know whether it was
"he piteously said" or "she piteously said."

What to do with the page?

I decided on the "F-file." I call it "F" as short for
"fugitive and ephemeral materials." The library policy
is to wait for these to accumulate, sift, and weather the
test of time. If we find more and more pamphlets on
a given subject, we finally bind them in cardboard and
string, make a brief catalog entry, and put the bundle
out on the shelf. Most of our collection of single-tax
schemes came together this way. The bulk of the
F-file is crank literature, or unrequited love letters—
depending on how you look at them. I filed Valparosi's
last page under the heading FRAGMENTARY.

It was good I looked. The F-file was crammed to
bursting. Every few months I have to take it upon
myself to weed the contents. There's no principle in
my weeding: I've asked around and no one has been
able to suggest any. The contents are all of doubtful or
unknown worth and no ready standards apply. So I
weeded at random. I removed: 2 confessions of perfect
crimes, 10 noble genealogies of obscure persons, 12
manifestos of the only true faith, 1 perpetuum mobile
design.

Now there was breathing space.

After lunch I was surprised to encounter Mr. Valparosi cooling his heels in the corridor.

"Just one minute—" he said.

"But . . ."

"One precious minute, one lousy minute. Spare one. Even the Mayor's got a minute to spare. So who are you bigger than the Mayor?"

"Well . . ."

"If you would step over here." He motioned me away from the water fountain and into the vicinity of a neglected alcove where a founder's bust stood.

Would he be asking for a handout? Should I go with him? Was this a stickup? Did I dare *not* go? The cold marble gaze of Jameson Adams Cornford gave no clue.

"What's up?" I ventured.

"Listen, friend. I got something I want to get off my chest, something to confess."

"Yes?" By now I was weary, an overlong joke.

"But first—don't you want to know what the title was?"

"All right. What was the title?"

"Guess."

"I can't. I have no imagination. You'll have to tell me."

"Tell me what you think of it. It was *Drowning with One Eye Open.*"

"That's very good, very dramatic."

"Wouldn't you automatically grab a book with a title like that? I mean—how could you help yourself?"

"Mr. Valparosi, what is it you want to get off your chest?"

"It wasn't thugs destroyed my book. I thought you ought to know the truth."

"So who then?"

"The dogs."

"The who? Whose dog set fire? Knocked over? Don't foll—"

"The dogs of doubt."

"You mean *you* did it? And then you give me a long sob story!"

"This is the sobbingest story of all."

"How could you destroy your own work? It's a kind of suicide."

"How could I do it? Easy. Eight rejection slips in a row, that helped. How did I do it? Easy as pie, right hand, left hand, that easy. The right hand proposes, the left disposes. Hey, that's not bad! Have to make a note of it—put it in a book someday. What am I saying? Only joking. . . . You turn me on, do you know that? You really do. I could tell from the minute I laid eyes on you, you're a guy that's easy to talk to. I bet we've got a lot in common. How about coming across the street for a cup of coffee? That dump you work in gives me the creeps. Closed-in like. It isn't a real office. How can you stand it?"

69

"Look, I told you. I've got work to do. No time to spare. And I don't find this much of a joke." I didn't. "How can you joke about it?"

"What should I do—weep?"

"See a doctor. Take care."

"Very nice meeting you, too." He waved me off.

As I turned the corner, I spotted him still standing as before, hands outstretched, palms turned up, not begging, although a stranger might have thought so. Not begging, no, but studying his hands, right hand, left hand, as if for the first time, as if wondering whether they had a use, whether to keep them or to chuck them.

When I came back to return Valparosi's last page, only moments later, he was gone.

Really gone this time.

There's one thing bothering me at the office lately. It happens usually when I leave my desk. I'm only a few yards away from the central cluster of desks, standing at the corporate authority file, checking format for corporate headings:

> Gt. Brit. Office of the gas referees.
> Gt. Brit. Office of the King's remembrancer.
> Gt. Brit. Office of the Masters in lunacy.

> Gt. Brit. Office of the parliamentary counsel.
> Gt. Brit. Office of the revels.

Office of the revels!
I itch all over.

> Gt. Brit. Office of the umpire (unemployment insurance)
> Gt. Brit. Office of the woods, forests, and land revenues.

My mind goes hopping away and back, like one of those red rubber balls attached to a paddle by a long elastic cord. The others gather at Arragan-Horgan's desk.

It looks like a huddle, although no one links arms and no one tries to break in. They are only cracking pleasantries, probably discussing something harmless and inane like MacFinster's distress when he discovered that some of the girls didn't have modesty panels on their typing tables.

They begin to laugh. It sounds like laughter, but it holds none of the kindliness of laughter. And anyway, there isn't that much funny to talk about. I've noticed Arragan-Horgan and Mary enjoying each other's remarks disproportionately, immensely. Each is feeling a release of energy in anticipation of the other's very thought, that's the way I reason it. (I know—their desks are only inches apart; they either have to put up with each other or shut up.) They're speaking to each other in code, enjoying the charm of a collusion, that's the way I *feel* it.

But then—I have Meg. She's in my camp.

●

Something *is* happening, something—dare I say it? —something hopeful. Meg seems to be changing, seems to be coming out of her shell. The promising signs don't go away. Chief among them is this: Meg looks me in the face, for the first time with focus, eye to eye. It's the first time she's acknowledged my existence in this way since her return home.

My sleep is much better these days. I still dream of a drunken boat, decked high with flowers, all glowing pinks and orange; the river is speeding; wherever the boat touches the shore, there is instant flame. It is a vivid dream. The little boat skims in and out of the conflagration unscathed, its crest of flowers high, fresh, and moist. I watch the boat glide, skim, and dart, as I watch a film charged with color; I am stirred with an aloof pleasure, then a distant thrill of fear. I dream a lot lately, but close to the edge, close to the threshold of waking.

My dreams are mappings with a domain that is all

shifting surface, no scale, no demarcations, only locations, punctures or mouth holes, where terror and lust are the sole inhabitants, and people are only the sites for these, only the tags. I lie imbedded in the texture of the dream as a worm in nature. In order to begin to dream, I must surrender all my baggage: my name, my sufficient reasons, the no-color of my hair, these things fall from me and others may grab them, as the property of the landed under a new egalitarian order.

It was early Sunday afternoon. Finding Meg asleep in her room, I let her be, momentarily forgetting the reason for waking her. Why should she wake? Why should she ever wake? The fact is, all women die after fifteen, although there's a universal conspiracy to pretend otherwise. Just when they seem to be blossoming, full and soft, with babies in the belly and babies at the breast, that's the festival of dissolution begun, the rosy flush of decay. Anyhow, I forgot my reasons for waking Meg, and, losing my own sense of prospect and destination, I wandered up and down the corridor, settling at last on the living-room sofa, where I fell into a light sleep.

I was dreaming of a library fire when the phone rang. I tried to cling to the dream.

It was my moment of truth. The fire raged; the fire alarm made the air bleed. I had chosen to stay behind with the books. The others, the most surprising people, people whose existence I had never even guessed at, surfaced and fled from the stacks like roaches from the woodwork, bent, wizened, with gray, dust-colored faces. MacFinster came forward out of a hidden corner. He was bare to the waist. On his smooth chest a tattoo in blue, a gothic "G" entwined with roses. He was wearing pedal-pushers of dark velvet and his legs were bare from the knees down, terminating in metal cuffs round the ankles and little wheels instead of feet, one on each leg, like sofa casters. I gave him a short push: he coasted, then stalled, arms waving. The fire licked his legs. A file clerk darted out from behind me. He was completely naked except for a chain of paper clips around his waist and an open book which he hugged below. A pretty boy, lifting his knees high, absurdly fig-leafed. The fire licked my hand, the fire alarm. . . .

At this point, I recognized the phone for the fire alarm and ran for the receiver, afraid suddenly of missing both worlds, afraid that I would reach the phone only in time to hear the final click.

It was Tim and the matter was so important that he had to see me right away. No, it couldn't wait until tomorrow. His delivery was telegraphic; no, he couldn't explain on the phone. I agreed to meet him outside the Eighth Street Bookstore, his home base. I also agreed to take the car, something I rarely do in the city, since parking is such a hassle. But Tim had to talk in private and his mother was at his place; and as for my place, it is full of ears, ears and echoes, echoes and ears.

We drove around in silence for a while, then took the bridge to Brooklyn. Once in a strange borough, we felt better. Tim began to chatter about this and that, nothing.

I found a parking place and turned off the motor and the lights. We sat in silence, his breath grazing my cheek. It was a quiet street faced with warehouses, their big ripple-front metal doors drawn like shades. There wasn't much of a moon. I could hardly make out Tim's face, but I knew from the rapid crossing and uncrossing of his legs that he was shuffling for a way to begin.

"Well, Tim, the suspense is killing—what's up?"

"Yah, that's best. I'll say it right out. Listen, Rich, I want— I'm going to get married. I've met a girl."

"Well, okay, that's understandable. After all, Meg— To be expected. And anyway, you don't need my permission."

"Try and put yourself in my shoes, Rich. I've been tied to a memory for too long. Years too long."

"That includes me, I suppose. I'm part of that memory."

"I think—under the circumstances—that this ought to be goodbye."

"That's it? Toodle-oo? Nothing left?"

"Uh huh, I think so. I mean it, Rich. What attracted me most about Meg was that Mona Lisa quality she has. You know what I mean. But it turned out to be blankness, not peacefulness, not anything resembling peacefulness. I made a mistake, that's all. It wasn't her fault. It wasn't my fault—a mistake. A mistake that cost me a big hunk of my life, let me tell you. Now be fair. How many years can a man go on talking to a wall? What I'm trying to get across to you is that I'm just an ordinary guy and no saint and no visionary. A blank wall is a blank wall, it's finally got to me. I'm telling you this just so everything's crystal clear. I want a normal life and I don't see why I should apologize for wanting something perfectly normal, something I'm entitled to. I think this ought to be the last time for us. Too many memories, Rich. Let's save the good ones, chuck the bad. I'm sorry. Don't you want to hear about the girl?"

No, I didn't want to hear.

I leaned back against the upholstery, too much blood swilling around, going nowhere. I should have thanked Tim for his loyalty all these years: I couldn't. I should have started up the motor then and there: I couldn't move. He reached over, roughly.

"All right there, Rich?"

I fell on his neck; I didn't mean to; it was limpness. I was water, others shaped it. He put his arm around my shoulder; something or someone strained me to him. I pressed my cheek to his, fitting myself close. I felt his ribs against mine, his heart opening and shutting—a fist, a bird, a fist.

A few minutes later, in perfect control, my mind a perfect vacuum, I started up the motor. I drove back over the bridge through the streets of lower Manhattan until we arrived at Tim's corner. There were no cars on the road and the road itself was a frictionless plane.

"Goodbye, Rich. This is goodbye." That's what he said, or I thought he said. It comes to the same thing. I was water, cool, indifferent.

●

I was running to work. A man cried out, "Don't run—you'll fall! Don't run—you'll break your knees! Don't run—you'll break your heart!" I ran from him as if my life depended upon it.

The budget squeeze is on; funds are being cut. Until the efficiency expert arrives and the new funds come through, the library has ceased to live but has continued to maintain a pantomime of life. Five student pages have disappeared without anyone noticing exactly when, two clerks . . . The acquisitions department continues to select books, to fill in the myriad order blanks, white, pink, green and yellow, to make out the invoices; they are as busy as spiders spinning, but the orders are never sent, the invoices are only filed away. The catalogers have begun to clean their desks and shelves, the old books moldering, the single obscure monographs flaking away into chips and dust, the inconvenient books, the casualties with missing title pages, all that was hidden under the stacks of shiny new books is at last seeing the light. What an exhumation! Moisture, fungal mottle, firebrats, book lice, wood roaches, bristletails, bread beetles, termites, fish moths, acid embrittlement, and time—time, all have been busy upon our buried store. Some of these crumbling books have been hidden away for as long as a decade and surprise the newer tenants of the room. The readers come and go as usual; business looks brisk; but the filing of a request slip is an empty formality. Only one book in four is ever searched. Some of the readers know this; they take their numbers and walk out the doors, as if the ritual alone sufficed. Some wait around, fanning through the pages of books on the open shelves, the encyclopedias, dictionaries and telephone directories: some have taken to reading the card catalog itself. Life goes on, but only a simulacrum of life; the blood no longer flows. Absenteeism has reached an all-time high. It's the tension and the busy work. We await the coming of the efficiency expert as if it were a Second Coming, as simple folk await the coming of the Messiah.

This afternoon, for the first time, I was able to read the motto on MacFinster's desk. It's the central inspiration, guiding all our operations in the room. I had heard about it, but I had to see it with my own eyes to believe it. I seized the first opportunity that came my way: MacFinster's phone was ringing and he wasn't in his office, so I stepped inside to take a message.

It stands next to his onyx pen-and-pencil stand with the clock inset. The plaque faces inward and visitors can't read it, so it's clearly meant to inspire, not to impress. It's laminated plastic done up to look like wood. Gothic script, and the words were culled from Scott's *Fortunes of Nigel*. (So it says, I wouldn't have known.) Thus:

> I have known a learned man
> write a thousand pages
> with one quill.

Heavy ledgers, MacFinster's mind.

●

It's raining on my way to work, a fine pizzicato of a rain. I am thinking of Meg's finest hour.

She's been chosen for the Miss America contest and

is standing in the second group of ten semifinalists! Moments ago she passed the bathing-suit contest and the evening-gown contest. In the evening-gown contest, since the girls chose the gowns themselves, something of their personalities was revealed. Meg's gown is sleeved and hooded, the only one. It is a traditional empire A-line gown of fawn-colored nylon organza with embroidered Alençon lace, deep, scalloped cuffs on the full sleeves, and edged with a satin panel that flows down the front of the skirt and encircles the built-in chapel train. The hood is also satin. Dramatic interest is achieved by wide crescent cutouts under her scented armpits and around her navel, where the gown is perforated in the shape of a rose. Her navel appears as a rose within a rose. Meg has blossomed miraculously for this contest. She has built up her pectoral muscles. She is still very slim in the hips; however, the judges are entranced by the new reversible girl-boy look.

Now she has been reselected as one of the five final semifinalists. The tension is something awful. Meg has taken her place on the second pedestal from the right. The girls are weeping with assorted emotions: strawberry, chocolate, and vanilla. The pedestals have rounded sides. The silken curtain descends in scalloping folds. Down it goes, over the five eliminated girls. To the left of the master of ceremonies is a tea caddy with five trophy cups of varying sizes; each of these girls will be a winner. Miss America will be one of these five, she is standing on one of these five pedestals—which one? There will be four runners-up.

On to the poise test. The girl on the far right pedestal gracefully dismounts. The other four girls also descend with elegance. They file past the cameras and are ushered into a star-spangled howdah. Then they are spirited away by four high-stepping firemen swinging the lacquered poles. The firemen are keeping time to a rumba beat. The test will be the same for each girl, so the others must not see.

Now for the poise test. An inconsequential question: a decoy. The real test comes when the girl is finished speaking and walks back to her pedestal. In her relief, the first girl gets snagged in her own feet; she trips over a deliberately misplaced microphone wire. And now a word from our sponsor . . .

The other girls follow suit. All—but one—grimace, flail, scythe the air. Each resumes her pedestal, shaken, wearing a crooked smile. All but Meg.

Meg alone has passed. She jumped nimbly over the sudden obstacle—and on seven-inch spike heels! Attago, girl! There was a tremendous burst of applause. Meg is always expecting traps, so she was ready.

She's always been a wary one. For years she went up and down steps by placing both feet on each step, a painfully slow way of getting anywhere, converting a flight of steps into a succession of many landings. That's her nature. Once in a great while it pays off.

Almost the winner now! Meg smiles, showing her

choicest teeth and a curling tongue; she lifts one knee, kisses it, lifts the other knee, kisses it. The provocation is too much. Bullets ring out. A scuffle breaks out in the back of the auditorium. The girls weep. Meg alone smiles and waves: she gives the two-finger victory sign, then the one-thumb up-your-ass salute. The crowd roars.

The girls are still weeping, but not one has deserted her pedestal. Meg has been an inspiration to them all. Now the pedestals gently, gaily rise, telescope upward. It must be a mechanism buried under the floor. The girls are lifted heavenward on monumental pillars, each a giant phallus. Slowly they ascend to the ceiling and beyond—up, up out of sight. The men in the audience faint. The women roar and stamp. The musicians have long since expired of ecstasy and lie limply draped over their drums and golden horns.

Farewell, Miss America! Farewell.

In point of fact, Meg is waging a hunger strike, trimming her down nicely to flagpole proportions, the latest look in elegance.

It's been four days now with only a little milk. I've told Miss Kay to stop urging. Enough of "Won't you have a forkful of this lovely cake, Meg? People in Bengal are starving, you know." A poor persuasion under the best of circumstances. We simply have to wait this one out. I've been through it all before. So let her be hungry for a week, let her go hungry for ten days. She'll lose some weight but she won't starve. When has she ever starved?

Does she suspect anything at all about Tim? Not a sign. And there's no way of knowing, no way of finding out without giving the game away.

●

Meg has been waking later and later each morning. Her skin is waxy from abundant sleep. She's started eating once again. It takes hours. She picks and picks, unravels the meat with her fingers, thread by thread, holding each to the light. The process of examination and selection takes as much as two hours sometimes, but she does swallow eventually and that's all I ask. Otherwise, nothing new, that is, nothing much doing.

I took her out for a walk by the edge of the park. We never got there. Police barricades were mounted along both sides of the avenue. I noted them. Meg said nothing. A parade? I raised the question—rhetorical. Meg said nothing. There were no cars in the street and the most outlandish people were milling about in the place of cars: rich girls in Salvation Army castoff coats, in the long skirts and embroidered pouches of nomads, young men dressed as the soldiers of 1776, as Edwardian dandies, nomads, they seemed to be nomads of some kind, children of no particular place, of no particular time. But Meg had seen this masquerade before, a hundred times before, judging from her face. She didn't bat an eyelash. Would nothing force her to speak?

Yet the cold wind suited silence. My words smoked into air, puffpuff, like the mere exhalations they most of the time mostly were.

Once, crossing the street, Meg clutched my arm. It was nothing, a double-take, of my own heart. It meant nothing. It was an isolated moment, nothing preceded it, nothing followed. Nothing but the very predictable paralysis. Meg froze in place, as if to annul the action, as if the action, any outgoing action, were a grievous lapse.

We seemed to be in the middle of a seasonal migration. Or was it an ambulatory convention of some kind? A march? Not a peace demonstration?

Yes, another one.

Some of the children had banners which they unfurled, others carried poster boards: love, power to the people, peace, flowerpower, free all political prisoners, free Angela, free grass, bring the boys home, down with the imperialist capitalist aggressor, out now, gay is beautiful, Jesus saves.

Minutes passed; Meg stood. As long as the demonstrators were marking time waiting for those ahead to move forward, Meg looked perfectly natural, a part of the scene. But it wasn't to last long.

"Form lines! We'll be going ahead in a minute now. Yoohoo, you! Step up, please." A youth with a white armband instructed the crowd to close ranks. He moved on down to the next group before finding out how we shaped up. Not very well, actually. A few semblances of lines formed, none of them very straight.

But Meg and I would soon be in the way. We would have to move away from the center of the crowd, off to the sidelines. It was a matter of only a few feet. A simple mechanical maneuver. The only complication was Meg—formidable.

I appealed to Meg with words—no result.

Words and gestures—unavailing.

It was time for desperate measures: force.

I tugged; I applied the waist treatment recommended by Miss Kay; I poked her in the ribs with my elbow; finally, in desperation, I stepped on her foot. No flinch, wince, flicker, not a glimmer of life. Meg simply stood and stared. Stared at nothing in particular. It was embarrassing for me, for me for Meg. Meg herself suffered no embarrassment. I glanced helplessly on all sides, tugged again, shrugged again, by way of informing the world at large that I was trying my best. My poor best. But there was no moving Meg when she didn't choose to move. She'd rather go to hell of her own free will than to heaven under persuasion. Maybe hell was just that: her own free will.

Since my concern got me nowhere, I tried non-chalance. Meg and I were simply spectators, on the scene. Granted, we were somewhat unusually placed: spectators in the middle of the fray. For the march was underway and, because we were motionless, we were creating something of an eddy around us. A few of the marchers were deflected, thrown off forward course and, for an instant, veered. But no one stopped to ask what we thought we were doing.

The factions passed us: the red-banner bearers, the white-banner bearers, the sober citizens of conscience in ritual penance, the four-letter men, a button vendor, six nuns, a mass of liberationists, the gay-and-proud-of-it holding hands, the united sisterhood of aggrieved womanhood singing and raising their fists in turn, a couple of amalgamated meat-cutters, flower children, a busload of matrons from Yonkers, hospital workers in paper caps, Maoists, the Attica Brigade, Socialist Youth, a marijuana contingent, students in beggars' motley (one carrying a sign that read "The Poorest Rich People in the World"), a man of slow dignity with immaculate white hair, dark suit, dean or deacon, trying to keep pace with the riffraff. The procession looked at first sight like nothing more than debris rattling along a beach, the shamble of systems before the cleansing wave.

Yet the crowd was marching in rhythm and chanting in one voice:

"What do we want?"

"Peace!"

"When do we want it?"

"Now!"

"What do we want?"

Over and over: the same hurrah.

It was the old one-two: loose step, lockstep. The crowd stormed by; few gave us a second look.

A girl in a cape presented Meg with a red chrysanthemum. The girl offered, hand outstretched, but Meg did not extend her hand to meet the flower. The girl shrugged, retracted the flower, went on.

The crowd was beginning to fray at the edges; it was thinning out.

I noticed a television camera panning the crowd. I saw, but didn't hear, a reporter sharing his microphone with a young man in a three-cornered hat. The young man was wearing love beads and a belt studded with bullets. I spotted another camera on a truck. The media people were present in force, getting the message but taking pains to miss none of the sideshow.

Did the cameras catch Meg? Scoop her in as one of the crowd? Or did even the grossest net filter her out as different, unassimilable?

The last remnants of the crowd were trailing by. It was hard to say where the marchers left off and the strollers began. A tiny woman walking a chihuahua. The little dog was encumbered by a knitted coat with satin lapels. The camera men had folded up and gone without our noticing exactly when. It was growing colder the longer we stood. My left foot was numb.

"Meg, must you stand right here in the middle of the street? Must it be just this particular moment?"

No answer.

More desperately: "They'll be taking down the barricades soon and the cars will be back, so you're going to have to move whether you like it or not."

Meg nodded her head and then said softly, "I was standing to a thought. Let's go now."

I didn't dare press my luck further and ask, What thought? Meg had confided in me, I treasured the fact. It was the first calm consecutive utterance from her lips in a long while, and I demanded nothing more.

But, like everything else hopeful, there was no sequel.

Meg sat and slept to every one of her thoughts this evening.

●

Miss Kay: Looks like a storm blowing up. What color would you say the sky is?
Meg: No.
Miss Kay: If the sky is No, is the earth Yes?
Meg: *You* said it. (*Rich laughter*)

Meg smiles often now and surprises me with her playfulness. She sings, ditties of her own making:

"Here comes the bride,
a finger in her eye."

And:

"Decisions, divisions, derisions . . ."

And, plaintively:

"Mortimer, Mortimer,
where are your marbles?"

This morning the ball dropped from her left hand. Abruptly she snatched it up, then ran the length of the hallway bouncing it with her right hand, schoolgirl fashion:

"A once An Apple
Met An Apple
Said the Apple
To the Apple . . ."

But is this sudden playfulness ground for hope? This afternoon some kids were jumping rope in front of the house. Two were turning the rope, two were standing ready to jump in, the others stood in a loose knot, waiting their turns. Meg pushed herself ahead of them all and flung herself into the center. I held my breath. My heart said, Stand pat. I was sure she'd get herself snarled. But no, her rhythm was perfect.

Attago, Meg! It was a full three minutes before she lost the beat. The kids began to mill and push. When I pushed them back to keep them from getting hurt, they began to shout and to scatter.

"Hey, what's the big idea?"

"What's going on?"

"I didn't get a turn, mister."

"Me either!"

One of the girls stared at me with large fear-bright eyes, then backed away with steps so jagged that she seemed to be tacking. I had to laugh. Looking into those hard little faces, faces smooth as pebbles, it was plain to see that they did not understand what was going on. Nor did I, for that matter, nor did I.

It was one of the most restless days I've ever spent with Meg, and she continued pacing all evening, long after I was spent. Tired as I was, I continued to follow her. From the kitchen to the living room. From the living room to the kitchen. Miss Kay entered the kitchen, stood for a moment, fingers drumming on the edge of the sink.

"What's the funny business? *Now* what's going on?" Her voice was hectoring.

"Meg is thinking about something, actively thinking. She is standing to her thoughts," I said, acting as interpreter.

Miss Kay threw me a wild look.

Meg laughed. "Um un. Oh no."

Signs of wellness: I'm taking stock. There are at least these gains: No resistance in being dressed. Meg is now almost feeding herself. I cut the food; she spears it and lifts it to her mouth. When she eats, the food splashes over her chin and onto her blouse, but that only means she's eating with more zest. She acknowledges pain when I insert the rubber ball in her hand every morning; this is a big change. (But the cramp in her left hand has not become less disabling.) She walks. On her own. With massive strides and semicircular sweeps of her arms, a swagger. (A burlesque of walking, more strut than walk, it is true.) Meg talks. Once in a while, a complete sentence: subject verb object. Even when she rants (strange incoherent babbles mixed with giggles and hisses) she's ranting audibly lately, as if she means to be heard. (Her voices vary as much as hats in a shop; she is only trying them on.) Topping all these gains, Meg has begun to converse. (Mostly with herself, I admit.) This evening I sat on the hassock by her chair, close enough to make out her stream of comment on the magazine as she leafed through it. "Yes . . . yes . . . no . . . yes or no . . . maybe . . . oh no . . . yes he can . . . can she? . . . hell, no, we won't go . . . my own voice . . . Meg . . . it's my name . . . no one ever calls me Maggie . . . must be crazy the one who stares at me insane that goes without saying . . . oh that's Richard, Richard the true Meg the false Richard the good Meg the bad . . . fungus among us. . . ."

Thinking it over, my little progress report disturbs me. Are *these* signs of wellness? The wellness of a budding four- to seven-year-old, maybe. I was hoping for . . . Never mind, I was just hoping. One thing for sure—I need a change. Tomorrow's my day off. I'm taking Sue out for the evening, dinner, a movie, and afterwards—we'll see. Miss Kay is in charge at home.

●

The haze was everywhere. I felt very drunk, although I couldn't have been all that drunk since I remembered minutest details, especially the sex parts of the film. They were so explicit that I remember telling Sue that it was no longer necessary to have a girl friend in order to enjoy a love life. She thought my remark fairly witty and giggled to that effect, but then, in quiet contradiction, nestled against my sleeve.

We stopped in at the Shamrock Bar and Grill. I remember a man shouting over the booth, "I'm killing time because it's killing me!" He had no face at all, only a mouth. Blooey lips. After my third Scotch, I could no longer see Sue's face—or was it Mary's face? I had meant to ask Mary but noticed my shirt cuffs were yellowed and one button missing at the last moment. Not that it should have mattered; it shouldn't matter, but it did. I'm not like Arragan-Horgan. Once, when Mary told him that his tie was frayed at the end, he simply smiled, whipped out a scissors, and snipped off a good two inches of it then and there. "No more loose ends!" he declared, and that was that. Arragan-Horgan has a gift for converting his every blunder into still another charming eccentricity. With me, it's just the other way around.

So it happened that I was standing at Sue's desk when I discovered how shabby I was, and, since I had paused there causing Sue to look up eagerly, I never made it on to Mary. Sue's sweet, if angular, face tilted like a rhombus. What could I do? There was nothing else for me to do: I asked Sue instead of Mary. After my third Scotch, it made no difference that I was sitting beside Sue, not Mary, no difference at all; all I saw and tasted was cobwebs.

"You're coming home with me," she said. "Since you're in no shape—and my place is closest."

"Yeah, that'd be nice. Sure, I'd like to," I agreed. Not wanting to take her to my place.

How we got there I don't know. I simply collapsed onto the sofa. She sat on the coffee table, perched rather than sat. She leaned forward on a diagonal over me. The slant of her body meant one thing: kiss. I didn't mind.

When I next opened my eyes, the lights were out—I must have dozed off—and someone was undressing, draping fabrics over a chair. Who? What had I done to cause this? There was some sort of lightweight cover over me—was it a tablecloth?

From under the tablecloth, I took a last deep draught of peace.

"Been here long?" I lifted my head. Someone was lying on top of me panting softly, begging for a bite of something.

"Hey, there, I'm not your lunch!"

She giggled and squirmed. My mouth was filled with the aftertaste of something, the aftertaste of a dream; it might have been any dream. I swallowed hard: did she taste it?

"Who's Meg?"

Pesky question, fizz in my ear.

94

"Richard, I'm asking you something. Who's Meg?"

"She's in my mind."

"You mean—you think of her all the time. You know you've been saying her name all evening. Is she very pretty? Do you love her very much?"

"We live together," I confessed, without going into detail. Leaving her to infer what she would.

She drooped on my neck, her cheek warm against it.

"Don't! Please don't! I've *got* to go—"

"Um . . ." was all she said.

She closed her arms around my neck, bringing on darkness. There was no shaking her off. She had found her object and was demanding congruence. A beggar's tyranny. I didn't need her; she needed me. 'Twas ever thus or vice versa, and if the condition is mutual, they die—there's nothing else for them to do.

In a tight spot, I turn philosopher.

This clinging was not what I wanted. Did she taste the paste? I buried my nose in her armpit, evading her breast which was poking like a snout, nuzzling me, tickling my mouth, seeking me out. What I wanted most of all was to sleep, the sleep of the newly dead. I was so hazy. The girl was feeling very lightly her fingers were furry the tips of her fingers creeping very lightly downwards over my body. Deftly, she plucked out my buttons and spread my seams. Flesh, it was flesh she was after. Mine. She was beginning to nibble, to pry with her tongue. She took my hand and directed it into a puddle of warm plush—flesh? Hers? Melting

95

gums. Numyums. Teeter? No, said the fox, his voice as small as peas in March. Hey.

She placed my hand against my own member. Between us, Vesuvius rising rising. Hey, hey—

"Hey! Cut that out—"

Instead of laying off, she touched, this time with her tongue.

I shot up, throwing her off. Her head nicked the coffee table.

"Are you hurt?"

No answer.

"I'm sorry, really I am. But I feel nothing, don't you understand?"

She said nothing, understanding for the first time then. I felt her stunned silence, the chill of her perfect comprehension. I took her head in my hands as a small token of atonement. Her lashes glittered.

"Is it because of—Meg?"

"Yes. Because of Meg." (Yellow, yellow, I'm your fellow.)

"Then I'm sorry."

"Look—there's nothing for you to be sorry about. And when we meet at work on Monday, we'll have lunch together because we're friends. Surely, pressed flesh means nothing, adds nothing, to our mutual regard."

"Huh? What are you talking about?"

"A man who wants your vote will. You press his flesh to see what he's made of—a complete stranger—"

"You sure you're all right?"

"A complete stranger will."

"Listen, forget it. You're tight, you better go home. It's my mistake. Do you think you can make it home all right?"

But I wasn't tight; my mind was clear as glass. I felt very masterful after near defeat, suave, supremely able to cope. In my new mood, I almost wanted the girl, now that it was safely out of the question. As she covered her nakedness, I watched her watching me. (No use, dear, I live in a cupboard.) My refusal had placed me on a new plane. There was a kind of awesome tenderness in her eyes now, no longer a nagging lust. This was a much better bargain, being so much less intrusive.

So our little seduction scene was over. I had preserved it from squalor—and from splendor, too—and it was over. The haze had lifted. It was time to go home to Meg.

Squeezing her hand, I made my way to the door. She stood in the hallway a moment, head bent. I felt dishonored, too, a man who turns and runs.

But it didn't matter when I got home. Only sleep mattered. I was slowly covered by a blanket of nothingness. Sometime later, the blanket became a hanged man's hood. I woke, heart racing, to find myself stewing in my own juice. I had just had a wet dream without a dream, without any companionable illusion of human comfort, not even a face, without benefit of desire or pleasure or any erotic imagery whatsoever. I simply rushed out of myself into the surrounding desolation.

•

Meg suspects nothing of what went on at Sue's place last night—or was it Mary's place? Mary was the one I wanted to ask. It doesn't matter whose place, my mind is wandering. The essential point is what happened. It is essential to keep hold of essential points; they are a charm against————. We try not to say those words in this house. It's not true what they say about my sister. I didn't break and enter her, nor have I ever mounted her, ever. She is seamless, sealed, no man's pouch, no vile receptacle. No, she's not like other women.

I expected glances and barbed remarks from Miss Kay this morning. Instead, she simply asked whether I enjoyed the film last night.

There's no question about it: Meg is beginning to look up and notice things. Lately she's been seeking her reflection in every glassy surface she encounters. Into my eyes . . . a slow smiling face. Into a car with full Simonize, into the fender . . . bodies billowed like spinnakers in a gale; over the trunk of the car . . . withered skulls, bodies in bloom; over the hood . . . cliffs of brows, bodies swallowed by some sea. . . . Meg has a single response to it all: a nonstop giggle. She's right, too. If you know how to look for it, the streets of this city are the corridors of a funny palace, admission open to all.

But that's not the point, the important point is this: Meg is beginning to look at the world around her. Also, I think she's beginning to want to confront herself—anyway, I hope that's what it is.

Not long after one of these walks, Meg turned to me with tears of anger in her eyes: "You read my mind, don't you? Oh, yes!"

I put out my hand and a tear fell into it. I couldn't have been more amazed if I had put my hand to her face and her eyelid had come away with my finger. There's no flow between Meg and the world; she doesn't secrete. Maybe my own hand put forth the tear —a kind of resin?

Or was it Meg? Was this the first flow?

All my attention was contracted in my palm, my palm rough as wood, setting for Meg's one tear.

No second followed. We stood face to face unmoving for I don't know how many minutes, so taken was I with Meg's one tear, so oblivious of Meg.

Her one tear flattened, evaporated, leaving a faint aftertouch of coolness in my palm.

The truth of the matter is—I am drowning in my own wastes.

●

Breakfast at the corner Automat. Even at that early hour, not yet eight, the place was full. At many of the tables old people were sitting over their cups of coffee, brown-paper shopping bags deflated between their legs, as if they had a full day's worth of marketing ahead. Later you'd see some of them on the public benches, tilting their yellow faces to a meek sun, a tropism, to prove they were still alive.

I set my tray down at the nearest empty table. I wasn't left alone for long.

"Do you mind?"

I minded very much.

"There's nowhere else to sit."

Why ask then? I wondered. She sat down opposite me.

I mumbled something conciliatory and tried to eat faster. A tropical bird, shrill and vivid, a tiny oldish woman with sky-blue hair. Eyes were green, be-feathered, and nestled in little pods. Her approach was about as subtle as an invasion.

I averted my eyes, shifting them from plate to wall, from wall to plate. Once, when my line of vision accidentally intersected with hers, I quickly put a pane of glass between us. She was someone, something curious, on the other side of the glass, and I peeped at her through the window of a passing bus. Almost human now, she seemed about to shrivel before my eyes. Scrawled across her face was a map of her sorrows, the lines all running steeply down. She hadn't rubbed the rouge into her cheeks well, so that the red stood out in two stark islands of color.

I must have been staring too hard. She inclined her head so that her face fell into shadow and began sipping her coffee. She sipped for a while in silence. Then she shunted her cup aside, crooked her neck, and inquired, "Are you bashful?"

No, I said, that wasn't it. I just liked to be by myself, alone with my thoughts. The truth is (I didn't explain) that every word I say ought to come kissed with a quarter's worth of postage, it comes from that far away.

She asked me about myself: age, occupation, schools and interests, like a job-application blank, seriatim, on and on.

"The reason I wanted to speak to you is that you look so much like my son. I mean—the expression on your face is the same. And you know, my staring at him annoys him every bit as much as it does you. And still, I'm always doing it, same as I did to you. Isn't that funny?"

She didn't mean haha funny, so I nodded gravely.

Next she pulled out a photograph of her son and urged it upon me. I refrained from crunching it between my teeth, but only barely. What was there to see? Two eyes, two ears, one nose—central, one mouth —futile. Futile. He seemed to be in some sort of uniform. Postal? Military? So? So what?

I looked again, harder. But all I saw was a postage stamp for a face, a grey stain for a face, lead-color streaks—hair? And his expression? Flat, flat. A taste of perfect nothingness. No possible resemblance! I frowned intensely, pinching my brow to show the woman how mistaken her comparison was.

But she had been talking for some time and was on to other things.

"—and already a good job at the Corn Trust Bank. They like him so well, they're sending him to school nights. He'll be a branch manager someday."

While she was talking, very quietly, so quietly, without changing her expression in any way, she brushed my sex with her hand. It was under the table so I couldn't see and she brushed me so lightly that, for a moment, I wasn't sure. But the second time there was no mistake. This time her hand lingered. I jumped up, snatching my coat.

"Get a hold of yourself!" I shouted.

And I ran.

In hoc mundo me extra me nihil agere posse . . .
In hoc mundo me

Mundome—

I took leave of my breakfast, eggs, toast and coffee by the revolving door. A busboy in a white jacket politely asked me if I was through. The way he asked it sounded as if he wanted a personal apology, but I was shaky and it was all I could manage to find the door.

I made it out into the street and into the light of the day where the buildings stood as they always stood.

No one ran after me and I stood for a while leaning against the wall of the building, comforted, eased by its sheer mass and immobility, the intrepidity of cement and steel, holding firm, never running away. I thought fondly of the little girl, digested in its foundations.

It was right foot, left foot, on the way to work. En route, I passed these signs:

Painted on a wall: a prick, huge, splendidly erect, flanked by the hemispheres. Making a bold heraldic design, triune, like a fleur de lis.

The word MOTHER chalked above it.

103

An eye, my left eye, floating in the window of a butcher shop. A tooth, my feral tooth, gleaming.

Lockstep, loose step, I walked on. As I passed them, the women of the street opened red and purple lips to greet me.

I made an effort to collect my wits.

At work, MacFinster said conspicuously in my hearing, although not directly to me, "Mr. Henken makes too many waste motions, too much time spent checking and rechecking. I've watched him. There's no excuse for backtracking. We just don't have that much time to spare." He was talking to Arragan-Horgan, or more exactly, talking *at* me through Arragan-Horgan.

Take note, Richard Henken: the time-and-motion man is on the way, any day now. Fair warning. I must curb myself, really I must. Nothing but essential points and essential motions from here on out, nothing devious or fanciful or stray. Can I stick to it?

●

As I walked down the corridor towards the staff room, I could hear Arragan-Horgan's unremitting yattattatta. As I came closer, I could almost make out: "a lay is a lay is a lay." I knew he was talking about Mary because he changed to "the whips, the hooks, the screws" the minute he spotted me.

"Greetings, Richard," he smiled broadly. "Fierce weather, I see. You look like the abominable snowman."

"I am the abominable snowman."

"That's more like the old Richard," said Arragan-Horgan. "You've been pretty dour lately. What you got there? Two books, I see. Never lose a minute. . . . One for each eye? Or are they blinders?"

"Oh, blinders, I guess. What you been talking about?"

"Women," said Simon, "you know—in general. Any opinions?"

"Subject's pretty broad—opinions? Should I?" I settled down to unwrapping my meatball sandwich. It was wreathed in steam.

"Her essential nature . . . surely you've observed." Arragan-Horgan, moralist, had just consumed a cold lunch. "A single case suffices for the lot, so you must have an opinion," he pressed. He'd finished his saltines, only crumbs remained, but the peanut-butter jar was still a fourth full and he hadn't brought himself to capping it.

"Why? What have you observed?" I was busy chewing.

"Woman is essentially double," he pronounced decisively. "Forked. In body and mind. That's her nature. What do you say?"

"Nothing to add, really."

"Then you agree? Or can't be bothered?"

"I don't know. I'm enjoying my lunch. There's lots of oregano in the meat. I like it that way." There was nothing much on my mind.

"O woman! How far thy tongue and heart do live asunder!" intoned Arragan-Horgan with deep feeling.

"Very prettily put," said I for the sake of saying something. "Who said it, do you suppose?"

"Truth, brother, who hasn't said it, what man among us? Doonoo, actually. Name escapes me. I'll have it in a trice. Think a bit . . . sixteenth century, was it? Seventeenth? Doesn't come. . . ."

" 'Down from the waist they are Centaurs, though women all above . . .' King Lear—how's that?" Simon put forward.

"To the point! To the point!" cried Arragan-Horgan. "To which I add the Uzbek: *Malum est mulier, sed necessarium malum.* Why so silent, Richard?"

I racked my brain, but could think of nothing to say in extenuation.

"Every man has a penny scepter in his pocket, it seems," I mumbled.

"Don't getcha, Rich," said Simon. "Care to explain?"

"Not really."

"Nothing more to be said on the subject? So soon exhausted? A closed case, then." Arragan-Horgan made a gavel of his jar. "Hear, hear, the nations agree, the ages agree, the authorities all agree. Amen, amen. Well, what shall we talk about now? Your silence, Richard, broken only by oblique references, gets me down. Silence kills, secrecy kills. Think about it. What can we talk about now besides the weather or politics, any ideas? Simon and I were in the process of inventing a game, weren't we, Sim?"

Simon nodded assent. "I'm off," he said.

That left Arragan-Horgan and me alone in the lunchroom.

"Game?" I trod warily. "What kind of game?"

"I call it *Double Trouble*. Or, in case there's already a trademark on that, just *Muddle*. Or should I call it *Cope*? The thing of it—what makes it different—is this: If you win, you lose. And if you lose, you win."

"And the point of the game—the point?"

"You mean the payoff? The why-play? A very good question. What *is* the point? It's a revolution in the basic premises of gamesmanship for one thing. Aren't you curious to know how it would work out? How simpleminded we've been in our clear wins and clear losses, and how brash the assumption of a clear desire to win! Why, take any life situation you please with real people facing real options and you've got *Double*

Muddle or *Double Double Trouble.* How to sell the game when life's full of it anyway—that's the real question. Oh, well, back to the drawing board. By the way, what games do you play? Or don't you ever play? You know, Richard, there's something I feel bound to say to you." He turned his blue eyes upon me. His eyes are so cold, they blaze. "You take life too fucking seriously, if you ask me. Has anyone ever mentioned that to you? You have a mortician's bowed eye and a mourner's shuffle. Does this Temple of Culture weigh down upon you so—or, you needn't divulge—is it matters—ah, how shall I put it?—personal?"

No answer required; in any case, Arragan-Horgan didn't wait for one. His talk's a fence: he puts it up neatly, slat by slat; neatly, he shuts you out. He went on to prescribe what I thought he would: a girl, in spite of her double nature. Our conversation had come full circle.

Afternoon. I was out at the public catalog, following a lead:

> Love's Excuse
>   *see* Ancient Wickednes; or Wicked Babylonia with her Seven Deadly Sinnes . . . Layd Open to the Eye of the World.
> Ancient Wickednes
>   *see* Marianna, an Idyll. Formed by an

English Hand.

Marianna

   see An English Hand

An English Hand

   see An Hue and Cry after the Fundamental Rights and Duties of Englishmen.

An Hue and Cry

   see Hymn to Wealth, a Satyr

Hymn to Wealth

   see The Clerical Arts Disclosed: Their Ways of Insinuation, their Artifices and Several Methods of which They Serve Themselves with a letter to Mr. Woolwiche, Challenging Him to Make Good his Slanderous Charge . . .

The Clerical Arts Disclosed

   see Bowersock, Timothy, 1791?

Bowersock, Timothy, 1791?

   see A Strange and True Relation of the Prodigious Multitude of Beetles that have Destroyed the Plants, Herbs, and Grasses . . .

A Strange and True Relation . . .

Prithee? I was caught in a web of endless cross-reference. Whither going? Clearly, I had lost the thread. I had started out in search of the works of Anonymous Hieronymous, pseud., when my eye began to wander. I lost my way at the first turning. The trouble was, the place was too quiet. So many bowed heads, a gallery of sleepers, each sequestered in a dream. Only once in a while you'd hear:

"Ihud. Ihud."

A concert cough, dry and circumspect.

A head would lift. A hand ruffle a page.

Then silence again.

Then scandal broke out.

"Sex fiend," the security man muttered as he led the culprit out, "a real pervert!" And the silence was shattered, the spell broken.

Life returned. Heads straightened. A warm flood of murmuring followed in the wake of the retreating figures.

The fiend wasn't much of a man, more of an adolescent, his face diddled with spots; he was slight, smaller than average. His fiendish eyes were hooded and cast down, fixed on his shoes upon which two little pocket mirrors intermittently flickered and blazed. He'd been changing his seat all afternoon, trying to get a peep under a skirt. The angle wasn't right. I don't think he ever got much of a view.

Meg was nothing this evening. It was snowing out and I took her over to the window for a view. I turned off the light so she could see more clearly, and we stood together looking out. Together we watched the slow sifting of the grains of snow, the soft piling of the dunes . . .

Before going to bed, I happened to glance in the mirror. My face *was* a perfect blank. I spent the better part of an hour making faces at myself, practicing love, hatred, anger, fear, envy, lust, grief, feeling none of them but giving a careful rendition just the same.

●

Saturday morning Meg and I left early for a walk. "Beautiful snow—isn't it, Meg?" The snow was slaking into dirty puddles. "Surprisingly warm out—isn't it, Meg?" The air was bright but rasping. "You're marching as if you're the leader of the band, Meg!" She was.

At once she stopped and began dangling her foot in a snowdrift.

"Get your foot out of that filthy snow right now, Meg!" The truth *would* out! Meg has a way of making sure of it. She laughed, shaking the scabs of soot-encrusted snow off her boot.

"You read my mind, don't you?"

Who said that? Meg? Sometimes she speaks with my own voice. I can't be sure. She turned to me and laughed.

"I've something to say to you," Miss Kay announced before I had a chance to hang up my coat.

"Later . . . later . . ." I wasn't in the mood.

She waited patiently until ten and then began again, as if for the first time.

"I've something to say to you."

I suspected something emotional, sticky. "Let's save it for the morning—shall we? I'm tired of chitchat." I spoke in the level tones of reason. As for chitchat, we hadn't said a word all evening.

She looked away sharply. Internal hemorrhage? Neither mouth nor eyes betrayed her state. When she turned to me again, her eyes were dry and focused evenly upon me. Whenever I look at a woman, I see a pair of eyes below her eyes. That's a cliché, I know, but I can't work myself free of it. Even with Meg, although I try to banish the thought, I see another face, the truer one importuning, floating beneath her exposed face.

Take Miss Kay: under her stiff white blouse, two inflamed eyes were staring at me, vulnerable, quick to shrink, quick to pierce, quick to spread and yield, tender. . . .

"Does nothing interest you but Meg?" She was talking in this peculiar squeezed voice. Her mouth was taut. "Can't you ever leave off talking about her? She's a sick sick girl. . . ." The peroration begins.

Begin . . .

The Barai are a stately race inhabiting a landfill on the southern tip of the Hoboken river. They are widely scattered. They do not live in cities, or villages, or even colonies. There is no family life. Stately and sovereign, each is a law unto himherself, having no ruler, having set no one Barai over another Barai, having no government at all, having in fact no need of one another.

The Barai are uniformly six inches high. There are no variations. Their skins are uniformly mottled in sympathetic coloring with the land they inhabit: they are uniformly piebald, gray, green, and gray. Their moods vacillate between extreme extroversion and the deepest, most depressive introversion. During their happy hours, the Barai extend their eyes far afield on stalks projecting from their tiny foreheads. They are multifaceted compound eyes, tiny radar dishes, minutely receptive. In anger, the eyes are also extended, but in quite a different manner: on broad, fleshy hammer stalks. The Barai have legs that work clumsily like oars, but no arms. No arms, no noses, no need for noses, since they do not hunt by sense of smell, nor are they attracted in mating by the savors of the opposite sex. They are themselves, each, both sexes. Self-sufficient, then? Almost, not quite, self-sufficient; they do have mouths. The mouths of the Barai work by an organic electroplate system as with certain species of fish; material for food, correctly charged, simply falls into them. . . .

"You don't help Meg and you don't help yourself by thinking and talking of nothing else—"

Go on, I'll bet you can't go on.

. . . The appearance of the Barai in a state of depression is very different. At such times, the far-reaching eager eyestalks invaginate, turn inward like the fingers of a glove, and only two slight hollow protuberances can be seen projecting from the bland forehead. The legs also retract. If despair prevails, the mouth loses its charge and it, too, involutes, the lips fold into the throat and sink deeply down, there to drink deep of some hidden store and, finally, in cases of old age, its own secretions. All the senses close in and the outer world diminishes to a point. The Barai dead is only slightly less moist than the Barai despairing.

So—how do they continue?

At maturity, which never comes before a hundred years, the single Barai discharges a single seed. If the Barai is in a state of exhilaration, the seed is discharged upon the ground and comes to nothing. If in a mood of despair, the seed is discharged into an internal chamber, there to flourish. . . .

"What you're doing is deceiving yourself."

People are different from animals—but how? Their throats are more exposed, is that it? No self-respecting animal would walk around so open to a jugular attack, so vulnerable.

The peroration was about over. Ringing coda. The upshot seemed to be this: Miss Kay was giving notice. "There—that's news to make you sit up and take notice! Something you can't tune out, Richard. Something you've *got* to face."

Said she'd be leaving sometime in the next two weeks. She's greatly offended by my calling her "Miss" when her name is Kay— "just Kay, don't you remember?" Talks as if she were my wife. Of course, she's been with us a long time, on and off, ever since Mother's last illness became grave enough to require a private nurse, and she feels, quite rightly, as if she were part of the family. But—wife?

The things you have to put up with in this world! The strain of living with Meg must have been too much for her.

Could it be that I married her and forgot about it?

I told her not to act rashly, but to think it over carefully. It was her decision to make. I thought I was bending over backward to be just, but she seemed to resent my effort at fairness more than any harsh words.

She'll be leaving me—all alone with Meg. That's really sad, I said to myself, really sad, sad, sad. . . . But the words unexpectedly came out with rather a nice tune. And then an echo, not so nice: how would Meg and I manage alone? How? How?

In point of fact, it would be hard to find another to serve in Miss Kay's capacity, whatever that capacity might have been. It was a new thought.

I went to bed and lay there, listening to the wind tapping the glass. But I didn't sleep.

On past midnight, a man cried out, "Help me! Help!" I raced to the window. Others must have heard him as well as I, for there were the repeated sounds of windows slamming shut, sounds regular as shots. Then quiet, quiet.

●

A letter from Judy, Meg's best—and only—friend, arrived today. She's living in Detroit and wrote to announce the birth of her new baby. A boy, name of Kevin. This makes three kids. I usually answer for Meg, writing how busy I am at the library. She thinks Meg is a career woman. I'm counting on Judy never coming to town. I don't know how safe an assumption that is, really. Judy moved out west in her second year of high school and she hasn't seen Meg since. So far so good. When they graduated from junior high, she wrote in Meg's album:

When this you see, remember me.

———

Remember me, you shall, you must,

Until your teeth can't mash a crust,
Then when you can no longer bite,
Forget me if you think it's right.

Yours till Victor Matures,
Judy

On another page, I wrote:

Here's to my sis Meg—
Too rotten
To be forgotten.

At that time I still hadn't fully grasped that Meg was different from other girls. I had my suspicions, of course. But Mother would explain them all away. "Meg is being naughty again. Some one of these days she's going to grow out of it. It's a stage," she'd say. "Meg is going through a difficult stage." Stage on what route?—I didn't dare ask.

I can't say when it was exactly that I began quite privately to wonder. Was it when she stabbed me with the rattailed comb? Meg was upset, Mother confided in tones of deep awe, because—here, she paused portentously—because it was "her time of month." She didn't own the month, I yelled back; it was just as much my time of month as Meg's. Mother had been waiting for just such a declaration of ignorance. It gave her an occasion she relished to sweetly invoke the mysteries of life. There was a certain oily tone of voice she used whenever she tried to convince me of something she didn't really believe herself, that something sneaky was really wonderful. She told me how women earned their estate by excreting their own blood. Poor creature, it sounded like a bad joke to me. And how primitive, how very savage and gory! Meg was suffering the shame of her animal nature, no wonder she was upset. She still looked like a civilized person to me. It was hard to believe. But it didn't change a thing. So, Meg was bleeding, filled with pain —so? Did she have to draw my blood as well? It was only a surface cut, luckily, only a line etched across my cheek, but she had narrowly missed an eye, my eye. What had I to do with her woman's fate? She acted as if someone had taken a swipe at her from behind or written a foul word across her back, she acted as if she had been double-crossed, as if I had double-crossed her.

Or was it after that? The time of her first dance? When she went to the senior prom, that was a worrisome time. Mrs. Brady, our neighbor, had found a boy to take her—Steven, a short, studious boy, too shy to ask a girl on his own. So he got Meg. Not that Meg was ugly or had a game leg; she was very pretty, in fact. She wore a long blue gown. It was almost transparent and speckled with tiny white dots that stood up like braille. I forget what they call that kind of cloth. Her shoulders were bare and I was surprised that the gown didn't shimmy off her down to the floor. No, the gown held: her chest stood out in two peaks. It was the first time I realized she had breasts, two of them. They must have sprung up one morning suddenly.

She wore Mother's rhinestone necklace and bracelet and her hair was marshaled in curls; they stood up in neat rows like regiments, wire-stiff with spray. Mrs. Brady had done the setting; Meg would have never bothered on her own—it was all Mother could do to get her to brush her hair even once at night.

Her slippers were silver, brand-new. Mother called her "a princess," and Meg really looked quite grand. Her eyes sparkled. I thought it was excitement, but maybe it was mischief. Maybe all that happened at the dance was nothing more than mischief. It's possible.

Steven shuffled a lot when he called. He swallowed the endings of his words, fumbled his rabbit's-foot key chain, and hardly dared to look at me. They went off arm in arm, pretty as an advertisement. I seem to remember Meg giggling.

Before ten, they were back. I remember the shrilling of the doorbell; when I am afraid sometimes, I hear it still. They were out on the step, Steven and another girl. Meg was between them. Steven was trying to hold his lip firm, trying to keep his chin from crumbling. His eyes were hard and brilliant.

"She ruined my whole evening," he muttered, "my one and only senior prom." It was plain to see he was feeling gypped. He handled Meg as if she were a piece of damaged merchandise.

Meg was a sight. Not a hair out of place, that wasn't it.

The girl explained.

Meg had gone to the powder room with the other girls to pretty up. With the others, she had dabbed her earlobes with cologne, penciled her eyebrows, powdered her nose. Then, when the others did, she took out her lipstick.

With her lipstick, she had drawn a huge X across her mouth.

When I asked her later why she did it, she said:

"X marks the spot."

Or was it the time before that when Meg posted the sign on her bedroom door and refused to come out at mealtimes. The sign said:

THE MEAT YOU EAT IS SEARED WITH PAIN

She had clipped the caption from the newspaper. It was from a political advertisement, the Hudson-Lis bill for humane slaughter. Meg avoided all food for twelve days, then relented: she ate everything but meat. Mother became an expert in curious vegetable casseroles. Then, gradually, Meg seemed to forget all about it. She began to eat enormous quantities of everything without even looking at her plate; she devoured meat and gristle and wouldn't have stopped at bones either, if someone hadn't taken the bones away from her.

"A stage, like I told you. She got over it, like I said she would," Mother assured me.

Or was it the time, ages and stages before the dance, when Meg was only a kid? I was six then, so she couldn't have been more than eight or nine. She'd been crying as if her heart would break—I forget about what. Then she ran off into her room. I tagged after her, I always tagged after her; it earned me the nickname of "Little Me-Too." I stood and watched Meg from the open doorway.

Meg was crying as before but, at the same time, watching herself in the mirror. I suppose that was already strange. But, if it was, wasn't it even more strange what I was doing?

I was watching her watch herself cry.

●

It was not much before noon when I entered Meg's room to see what was up. She was lying on the bed, face reflecting the ceiling, hands folded over her belly, her legs spread out in a V, the knees bent upwards like the struts of a roof.

121

Between those struts: a briar patch, a rabbit hole, a vat. I speak of what everyone knows. Her posture was an invitation and a mockery. With every muscle she urged entry.

Slowly but gently, I pressed her legs flat and together, then pulled her skirt over them. I took her arms and tugged.

"Here we go—upsy daisy—"

"What do you want from me?" she snarled.

A very good question. What was it? What *did* I want from her? And then I noticed that my hands were shaking.

With all the patience I could muster, I said, "I'm Richard—Rich—your brother, as you know very well. No more fun and games, Meg, I'm losing my cool. You know me well enough. I don't want anything *from* you, I haven't come to take anything away. I've come to bring you something. I want you to stop wasting this beautiful day. Your whole life is slipping away while you lie here on your back, staring at the ceiling."

Meg turned over on her side, face to the wall—blank to blank—her back to me. I decided to step out for a cigarette.

"I'll be back," I warned her.

But I didn't want to go back, not ever. Cold, listless, I entered my mother's room. There I watched the shadows dart and nibble, fish-finger, the walls. The room seemed huge, cavernous. It was empty, except for Miss Kay's trunk and valises, and when I paced the bare wood, the floor gave back my footsteps "higgledy piggledy higgledy piggledy" again and again, as mirrors on facing walls reflect, within and within, endlessly.

My life was full of echoes, too. There was more and more space as time went on, fewer people. My one constancy was Meg. And if she were to fail me—what then? Meg wasn't to be counted upon. No one knew that better than I did. But Meg *must* get well. It was up to me. No one understood her as well as I did.

I felt my mind running on like a rocking chair left out in a storm; the rain and wind lashed at it and it went galloping faster and faster, madly, nowhere, in place.

The only thing really wrong with me was eyestrain from the kind of work I did, all the little dead letters. All those eyetracks. How many miles of print did I travel over a day if you stretched the letters end to end? And all of it leading nowhere in particular. It was no wonder my eyes bothered me. I kept telling myself that my eye trouble was a least ailment among the least of ailments, but, little by little, least by least, it was wearing me down. There was always a tugging mid-brain. My two eyes couldn't seem to work together any more but each worked for itself so that I often saw double, a montage, a flat double exposure; there was no fusion; I'd lost my vision for depth. Surprising how a minor irritation such as eyestrain, or an imaginary crustacean in the ear, how something as small as an itch or hiccup or tic, could demoralize a man.

I passed the mirror; it returned my face to me: ashen. Was that really *my* face?

It must be a strange face because people rarely looked at me directly, eye to eye; whenever they did, they ended up squirming. Peeping along a slant, they must have seen what I saw then.

A remarkable face. Not another like it.

My face looked like a composite photograph.

Spliced. Cleft down the middle and spliced again, but badly. One eye squinted, the other gazed. One eye gazed, the other squinted. One corner of my mouth smiled, the other leered.

That's how it was: one side of my face was surely blabbing on the other, backbiting, fibbing, spreading outrageous slanders or, at the very least, giving away my best jokes in advance.

Not long afterward, I did as duty demanded, returning to Meg's room. Did she notice my face? I made a point of showing it to her only in profile, exposing only one half at a time. She seemed not to notice. She rose from the bed with seeming willingness. Whatever had been troubling her earlier was forgotten. If she hadn't responded then, well, I don't know. Slipping on her sweater, I noticed her right hand. It was folded over, intractable as a rusted hinge, her thumb a latch. I held her hand in mine for a moment, warming it, easing it. But as soon as I let go, her hand drew together as before.

So much for Meg's good hand, her last remaining hand—

Speak to Dr. Grey, that was all I could do about it. I inserted the rubber ball in her left hand, as usual. There was the usual resistance and pain.

The day was no longer beautiful. It had turned gray, inside and out. I had spent all my energy in the business of getting Meg up out of bed and, by this time, neither of us wanted to go outside. I asked Meg if she wouldn't try some piano exercises for her right hand. I hit a note and Meg tried to repeat it. She responded by striking the requested note with the middle joint of her middle finger. Without unfolding her right hand, the total effect was a blurred resonance. I didn't want to discourage any outgoing action, any attempt at expression on Meg's part. So I combined notes and Meg combined fist strokes in response. Until Miss Kay entered:

"Would you please cut out your awful clanging! After all, I have nerves too."

No sooner said than Meg rose from the piano bench. She had forgotten herself and her illness just before. As if to apologize for it, she deposited herself in the nearest chair and became at once a statue. She stared at her spoiled right hand for the rest of the day.

I phoned Dr. Grey to ask about Meg's latest symptom—was it some sort of muscle tetany?

He didn't answer my very specific question directly, but said instead, "Matters certainly seem to have gotten out of hand, Richard. I'm going to arrange for a complete checkup including a neurological. You'll have to come down to the hospital as soon as I get the okay—hopefully for tomorrow."

●

Although it was one of Miss Kay's last evenings, I had to go out for a drink. I keep nothing in the house because of Meg.

Miss Kay watched me bundling up without saying a word. Her lips were white with compression, the lips of the righteous.

In the street, the snow was coming down in gobs of darkness. I turned in at the first lighted sign.

Inside, it was warmer, summer in fact, the golden rankness of beer. Still warmer with a glass in my hands. Beside me, crumpled on the next stool was an old man trying to smoke. His eyes were only half open. Some sort of tunnel . . . curious . . . he studied his sleeve. Something trapped in it, alive, unstrung. He couldn't seem to reach his mouth, although his hand set out four times to make the journey. His fingers held the cigarette expertly: it was not a tremor, it was only that the space between the hand and the mouth

126

was so unstructured. He began to structure the space, to establish landmarks. Slowly, painfully, he raised his hand until it rested on the ledge of his shoulder. From his shoulder to his ear, the way was not far. He established contact with his ear, put his thumb on it. Using his thumb as a pivot, he rotated his hand a quarter-circle clockwise to the chin, and the corner of his lip was accomplished, the connection forged. He took a deep draught of smoke. Then his hand dropped down to the counter and, for a minute, his whole body went slack, he seemed to sleep. Only a minute—and once again his hand began the ascent, the terrain as unfamiliar as before.

I couldn't help staring, wondering and fearing at the journey of that hand. How could a man become such a stranger to himself that he couldn't find his mouth except by external signs, couldn't remember where his mouth was by feeling it from within? How could it happen to a man? Was it drink? Was it drugs?

There was no one stirring when I returned home, not a light burning. All asleep? Or playing dead? I hadn't been gone an hour. Actually, I hadn't even finished my first drink, only warmed my hands on the glass and studied the man beside me. Now I was cold.

The house was so still. It would be a long night; I was miles from sleep. I turned on the radio. I could listen to the radio all day and all night even if it emitted a steady stream of sirens, anything but the silence. Once, I listened to an entire programming day on the radio. Continuous input until I wondered what I was putting into.

Now I waited for morning. The chairs, tired of standing, shifted from foot to foot, they spread like stains. The ceiling began to slope, then heave. . . .

Miss Kay was the herald of morning. "What you been doing sitting up all night? Couldn't sleep? Are you ill? Tell me if you are." She laid her palm across my forehead and, for once, I let it be. "Maybe it's flu—that damn fool walk in the snow. Something not right about your eyes. Do you have a headache?"

"No, I'm fine, just fine."

Meg and I finished breakfast in record time. We bundled up and left. The appointment at the hospital was for ten.

From the hospital grounds, the meshed windows seemed dim, revealing here and there the silhouette of an inmate standing motionless in an unlighted hall. There were no screams, not a murmur of life.

I had to pass through some strange corridors to get to the EEG room. The walls were yellow. (Decorator colors: red walls to blast the despairing into life; blue walls to subdue the manic . . .) They had probably

128

taken a survey to decide on the yellow. The color that offended least, or something to that effect. But it looked like the cosmetics of the dead to me.

The corridors were peculiar, open in one direction only, more conduits than corridors, they led past day rooms, night cells.

A big fellow stopped me. He was wearing a Mighty Mouse T-shirt under the gray hospital bathrobe.

"Hello," he said, "I'm God."

Was there a rejoinder?

"Which pocket? Which one?"

Which pocket what? He was asking some question of me; some answer was expected.

"The right pocket is Life. The left is Death. I'm going to take some Death now, a little Death." He glanced at me from the corner of his eye to check whether I was duly impressed.

Then he extracted a bent cigarette from the left pocket, and fumbled again. I gathered that matches were not allowed and offered him a light.

"What's in the Life pocket?" I ventured.

"Numbers . . . the Book of Numbers." It was a small blue memo pad with a spiral top, the kind in which kids scribble their homework assignments. He read a few numbers aloud, checking them off with an imaginary pencil.

There was a pattern to these numbers. What was it?

Finally I grasped it: "Phone numbers!"

This time, they tested Meg alone. It took hours. Years ago, when I took Meg to the hospital for the first time, they had me stand by and watch because Meg wouldn't cooperate on any other terms. The nurse had read from a looseleaf book full of questions and blanks.

The first page was marked ORIENTATION. There were a number of boxes. The first box was labelled IN PLACE. The second was IN TIME, and the third was TO PERSON.

"Meg . . ." the nurse had begun very gently, "can you tell me where you are now?"

She repeated her question, but Meg had only looked down at her shoes.

So the nurse answered her own question. "This is a hospital, Meg. Do you know what we do in a hospital?"

"Hurt."

"Not hurt—help, Meg. Heal. This is a hospital. A hospital is to make sick people well."

That took care of PLACE. The nurse went on to the next box.

"What's the date today, Meg? Can you tell me the date?"

Helplessly, softly, unsurely: "Tuesday?"

"No, Meg. It's Thursday, December sixth. I bet you know what year it is."

Meg looked down at her shoes.

They went on to the next box.

"Can you tell me who I am?"

"Police?"

"No, Meg, I'm the nurse. I'm the head nurse here. You're going to like it here, Meg. My name's Mrs. Merrykin—Marjorie Merrykin. Isn't that a funny, happy name? Do you remember what I do?"

"Hurt?"

"Not hurt—help." Nurse Merrykin pointed to the other nurse present. "Do you know what *she* does?"

"Helping."

"That's right, now you're catching on. I've got a feeling you're going to get well here, Meg. You'll be better in no time. I bet you don't even know that you've been sick. That's the first thing to face. We're here to help you. Felicia, come up and say Hi!"

Felicia came up and said, "Hi, honey."

"This is my assistant. Her name is Felicia DeRosa and she's helping, too. I just know you're going to get along fine."

By then, it was lunch time. We went down to the cafeteria where the visitors ate. In the afternoon we went back for Higher Intellectual Functions with the visiting psychologist.

The psychologist's name was Miss Punch. She spread out some drawings on the table in front of Meg:

A baby caught in a cobweb.

A rooster with small antlers.

A man walking on two legs through a snowfield, leaving a trail of left footprints only and crutch points.

A street lamp, half submerged, shining in the middle of a lake.

A bouquet of fingers and ferns in a vase.

A duck with one webbed foot and one cleft foot.

An eyeball, fringed with lashes, on a stalk; a bee alighting.

A table setting, complete with wineglass, flowers and fruit, knife, spoon, plate, pistol and napkin.

"What do you think of them—of these pictures?" ventured Mrs. Punch after an interval.

"Pretty," said Meg. "Wish I could draw."

"See any one you especially like?" Miss Punch persisted.

"No . . . they're all pretty."

Miss Punch glanced at me, a glance deliberate, purposeful as the swipe of a broom. Then she went on.

"I want you to tell me, Meg, what you think these sayings mean. Listen carefully and think. Remember —don't tell me what you think I think, tell me whatever it is you really think. It doesn't matter if it sounds silly. Okay? Here goes."

"Birds of a feather flock together."

"Us," Meg replied instantly.

"Us? Which us? Us how? Won't you explain?"

Meg looked down at her shoes.

"Don't be bashful, Meg. I think I know what you

mean. You mean we have more in common than we have differences. That's very true, Meg. Very true.

"Let's try the next, shall we? You catch more flies with honey than with vinegar."

"That means you," said Meg. "You is what I said."

Miss Punch didn't press for further explanation; she wrote down three words and went on.

"The tongue is the enemy of the neck," she said.

"Hah!" said Meg, smiling this time. "Always thought so."

"What's that?" cried Miss Punch. "Private joke? Won't you share it with me?"

Meg bit her lip.

"No? You won't share it with me? I'll go on, then. All right, I'm going on. A golden hammer breaks an iron door."

"An iron hammer breaks the golden door," said Meg.

"That's clever, very clever. What do you think of when you think of a golden door?"

Silence.

Miss Punch droned on. . . . "Many are called but few are chosen." No answer. "The hot coal burns—the cold one blackens. Yes? Make yourself honey and the flies will eat you. Well? It's a dirty bird that fouls its own nest. He who rides a tiger cannot dismount. Don't pry a stone with a sword the mouse that has but one hole is soon caught a threefold cord is not quickly broken—"

"You're insane, that goes without saying," said Meg imperiously. She stood up.

Miss Punch also rose, pressing a buzzer on the panel under her phone as she did so.

Meg turned to me and said quietly, "Rich, let's go. C'mon, let's get out of here." She took my hand.

I felt her hand on mine. I felt leather. I felt nothing. I did nothing.

I stood in place, locked in betrayal.

An attendant entered. Meg's voice rose, shrill, breaking: "I'd like my bags now, James. I've decided to check out now!

"My bags, please—and turn in my keys for me, will you? Shut your face, Rich—wipe that ugly smile off —I'm leaving you!"

Had I been smiling?

"This way, miss," said the attendant, "I'll show you the way." He graciously offered his white sleeve.

"All alone, Rich, all by your lonesome, you don't know what that means. You'll find out, just wait. You'll have to sleep on your own hand from now on—"

That did it! They couldn't take Meg away fast enough for me then. Furious, I felt the heat rise to my cheeks. Would these people read it as a blush, a haze upon an unmasking? Everyone was staring at me. I could have joyfully throttled Meg. Only wait a bit, I would have my revenge.

"Lap it up, Rich! They're really dishing out the slops here today. . . ."

As they went off, arm in arm, Meg said to the attendant, "Let's go, dear. That Richard is some schmuck!"

The examination had seemed to be over. I was amazed that they had failed to ask the essential things: whether she ever vomited strange things—hairs, broken glass, beads, pins, pebbles, or whether she blasphemed on a regular basis, or whether, from time to time, she ever emitted the cries of a beast—bleated, barked, or brayed.

It was after they led Meg away—those years ago— that I had committed my final act of betrayal. I placed at their disposal a pearl, Meg's last letter to me. She had written it less than a week before. She had been trying to live on her own at the Fairfax Hotel for Women; she had been looking for a job. "Dear little Rich," she began. She always called me "little" because I was younger, even though I'm just under six feet; she used to call me "pretty," too—why, I'm not sure. She told me that women were the secret side of men, and men the secret side of women. I examined myself in private: I had tits, they troubled me. No doubt about it, they were paps, not badges of merit, not wens. What were they for—not meant to suckle? Ornamental? Not very pretty. Vestigial? Had I been a woman in an earlier life? Meg used to tell me all sorts of things that made me dizzy, made me wonder whether my head was up or my feet were. Her last letter was sad.

> Dear little Rich,
> I like to keep my house clean as you know but they won't let me. Actually it is only a room not even a room a closet a hundred other closets like it in the hall but that makes it all the more important to keep my house clean. I don't talk to anyone as I mentioned in my other letter last night and I don't know how it is they know so much about what I am up to. What I mean by they won't let me is I can hear them gnawing at the walls here, scribbling all over the window and making designs on me. I don't want to have anything to do with them. It must be the Park doctors. Please come and take me away.
> Love and lonely,
> Meg

By the time I got to her it was already too late. It could have been minutes, days, months, years too late —what difference did it make? Too late is final. Meg had put her hand through the window of her room after writing the letter; the window had been closed.

And that was more than a decade ago, the first time I took Meg to the hospital. Ancient history by now. This time I knew nothing about the testing going on. A nurse came into the waiting room. She summoned me aside. She brought news.

Meg wasn't coming back with me; she'd have to stay. I'd have to face Miss Kay alone.

I followed the nurse down a long corridor. I entered Meg's new room, a yellow room. They had her between tightly drawn cold wet sheets, the pack treatment. She closed her eyes when she saw me coming. They had painted her face yellow, the eyepits blue. Mrs. Harte, the nurse in charge, explained: "This time, I'm afraid it's going to be a long stay." The nurse peered deeply into my eyes; the pupils were very wide. You could tell that she was heavily aggrieved. "She bit me, you know."

Such, such are the crimes . . .

It was evening before I knew it. The rest of the day somehow slipped through my fingers. I remember a parched throat—mine, sedation in daylight . . . no dreams. Then morning. But this was another morning than the one I was in when Meg and I . . . Why couldn't I remember? Miss Kay insists that she found me standing on the threshold of the door to the apartment pleading with some people she could not see:

"Everyone going so soon? Leaving so early? But we have so much more to say to each other."

That's what she said I said.

Have I come that far? So far that there's no one for me to talk to but the wall? These days I never think of Sue. We never did have our luncheon date. At work, she has taken to avoiding me. It doesn't matter anyway: Mary was the one I wanted to ask out. And as for Tim, it really was goodbye that time. Valparosi —Pinski—I think of them sometimes. Not often. Little by little, the stage clears. Until there's only Meg and myself, myself and Meg, sitting across a table from one another and tapping spoons (having no knives, no forks allowed), tapping our spoons against our glasses which are not glass.

It disturbs me—having no memory for what went on yesterday, not having the slightest inkling of what Miss Kay is talking about. All I know for sure is that I've been bedded down for some time. For some time I have remained in a state very like sleep, only quieter.

●

"Good morning, it's seven o'clock
On a rainy Monday morning
In the greatest city in the world."

Good morning to you. It's my clock radio floating on the waters. Everything is floating on the waters. I am a lotus, a floating sphere. . . .

> "Ladies: for the next sixty seconds, I want every woman who colors her hair to run her fingers through it."

I run my fingers through my hair, three times to make sure. No, I do not color my hair.

> ". . . there's a tie-up on the East Side Drive between 125th and 127th streets due to rubbernecking delays. Squeeze over to your left."

I am sorry for my delays: my legs are rubbery, my hands are very heavy.

> "Hari Krishna Hari Krishna Krishna
> Krishna Hari Hari
> Hari Rama Hari Rama Rama Rama
> Hari Hari
> Hari Krishna Hari Krishna . . ."

Interference from outer space. I snap the radio off. Yes, I'll be up—just a

What's this? One of Meg's queer jokes? In the half light, out of the silence, a pair of soft fuzzy slippers with no feet in them come scudding across the floor, slippers woven of emu feathers, human hair, and string, sent out on the trail of a departing soul.

Ready when you are, Meg. Just a sec.

Miss Kay just entered with a bowl of oatmeal, thermometer, and bedside manner. She rattles the pills in the paper cup: blue, green, and yellow. "Sunshine pills," she says. I thought she was supposed to be on her way out of my employ. She hasn't brought the matter up and I'm not going to mention it until she does. She's a very good nurse indeed, and I wouldn't want to lose her. According to Miss Kay, I've been "out of it" for three days. That means I left Meg at the hospital on Friday. I remember now.

Miss Kay also insists, although rather too vehemently (as if she were trying to convince herself) that I am "looking really better."

I ask for my shaving mirror. Leave it here beside me, please.

Really? Am I looking really better?

What a strangeness the tongue in my mouth, a fat fish, isn't it? I have this habit of watching myself, studying my reflections. Some thin, some fat, some false, some true. In fact, my life is nothing but a procession of mirrors. What with my limited mobility and lowered prospects, what else can anyone expect? There's no help for it, nothing for me to do but reflect, reflect, reflect, until my own tongue lies like meat in my mouth and the hair on my head creeps like an alien vegetation. My own name sounds Turkish to me. And what's this? Here, in the middle of my forehead, my eye, a mollusk. I live here and must live here, cased in this leather, till I—

It was Dr. Grey, voyeur of the human spirit, peeping from the doorway. He entered without knocking. He drew up a chair without being invited. Looking perhaps for the mote in my eye, or maybe for maggots, he peered intently into my face. When I stared back at him, his two eyes coalesced, not in a soft kissing blur or shadowy floating fish, but in a single corneal rind, hard, bright, more speculum than eye, more barrel of a gun than speculum.

"Not so close—might bite!"

"Ah, Richard. Jesting for a change!"

"Who are you, anyway? The police?"

"You are joking, aren't you?"

"Yes, of course, you're the doctor. Helping, not hurting, eh?"

"Have you been feeling well, Richard? Been confused?"

Kissing . . . that's how it began. I'd been kissing someone and it made me dizzy. That's why I mixed up the accelerator and the brake.

"It was a man—ah, you guessed that!" He'd just told me he was going to marry someone else. "You're right—I don't feel well. I'm trying to stay as lucid as

I can for as long as I can. For as long as I can hold out. Not much longer now. I'm trying my best."

He listened in silence most rapt.

"How's Meg, Doctor?" I began again, more carefully this time. "The other doctors must have phoned you by now. What did they say? What about her hands? How am I to get her to use them?"

"Say—hold your horses." Dr. Grey was all method. Let's see how you are first." He was stalling. "Now then . . ."

"Aaahhhhh . . ."

Hands over my body. "Feeling better?" he asked, jabbing my liver.

And I answered, "Yes."

A nod a smile a smile a swallow.

"A little nervous exhaustion," he pronounced after a brisk testing of my reflexes. "Nothing to worry about if you do as I'm telling you. But you need sleep. I can't insist enough on the importance of sleep. You need all the sleep you can get, young man."

"But I've gotta get to work by this afternoon at the latest. My desk! You should see it—what a mess! I can't miss any time now. We're about to be—"

He wouldn't hear of it.

"And anyway, you haven't told me about Meg!"

"Richard—Richard, isn't it about time we stopped denying the facts?" The good doctor said "we" as if there had been complicity before, and our collaboration was henceforth at an end. "I've played along with you so far. As your doctor, I warn you—your fantasies are growing out of all bounds. Soon it will be too late. You know very well your sister is—"

"Don't say it!"

"Aha! Don't say *what?* Go ahead, Richard, tell me what it is I mustn't say! You see, you *do* know. She's a shell. Hopeless. Empty. And you know it. And you . . ."

I didn't hear a word he said. I heard, but it didn't mean anything. It meant, but it wasn't true. A shell? Not a doodle in my dream box? Dried up? Outstare the sun, would she? Was it true—was I ill? With this charmed life I'd been leading? Dyspepsia after a banquet of nectar and ambrosia, such lovely curds? Tsk, how ungrateful.

It is very nice to think the world is full of meat and drink. . . .

It is very nice to think.

A shell?

And if she was, what had changed? Nothing. For a while, when she went back to the hospital, I stopped bringing breakfast into her room in the morning, that was all. For a while?

Ten years? For how long had I been pleading?

"Do you remember me, Meg?"

"Meg, what's my name?"

"What's my name, Meg?"

"No, *my* name isn't Meg, it's Richard. I'm Rich, your brother. I know you're fooling me, you remember. What's my name, Meg?"

It was Dr. Grey sputtering on: ". . . a shell and you know it. She's hopeless. But you—you're a different story. You're not hopeless—not yet. You've lost ten years, Richard, ten irreplaceable years of your life. Your young years, the best ones. You don't know what youth is; it only comes once. No one's going to give these wasted years back to you. Think, think of the waste. Give her up, Richard, don't throw good money after bad. You've done all you could. Add up your losses and call it quits. It's the damnedest thing, the way no one in your family would ever admit the facts. Facts, Richard, they have a way of turning up! Face up, Richard! You can deny the facts for only so long and then they begin to deny you. You're tired, aren't you, awfully tired? Tired of fighting the facts. Even a man of metal couldn't go on as you have. Even metals fatigue."

He was talking fast and loud now, as if he were trying to drown out a disputing voice.

"I'm going to work in an hour—you'll see!" My mind was made up. Dr. Grey's flight of ideas seriously worried me. He was a deeply disturbed man, that was obvious. "*You* need a rest," I suggested. "I'm getting up."

He frowned. "Nothing doing. I've ordered rest, complete bed rest. You need further examination."

"You can't test me—I'm a man of unmetered brilliance. I come from a larger life, you can't judge me!"

"The hell you are, the hell you do," said Dr. Grey, very cool.

The only question was, How could I enjoin my legs to move? It was no joke. I couldn't remember the difference between right leg and left, the separate networks, the chains of command, so how could I get one to move first?

"I've no warrant to restrain you," Dr. Grey said calmly. "But I'll be seeing you sooner than you think. Of that you may be certain." He rose with a little nervous jump, index finger in the air. "Unfinished business!" He wagged his finger in front of my nose. "Goodbye for now."

"We'll see about that!" My legs, both together went flying over the bedcovers. I catapulted myself out of bed.

●

No sooner had I entered the office when Mac-Finster nabbed me.

"Richard, for the last time, I'm warning you. Your desk! It's an eyesore. Everyone has shaped up but you. What's the difficulty? I don't see it."

If only I had one more drawer . . . I made a last desperate effort to yank open the drawer that was jammed. No go. Keep cool. Play it cool, Rich. Study the situation, all angles.

Very calm, I removed the drawer above it and rubbed my finger along the runners. A wad of paper, flattened, was wedged between the runner and the edge of the bottom drawer. I pried it loose with my scissors and was about to junk it when I noticed it was scribbled over in a minute calligrapher's hand. I felt a warm glow of discovery: I love things like this, eavesdropping, peeping through half-drawn shades, messages in bottles. I unrolled the paper; these were no random jottings. It seemed to be a testament of some kind.

HISTORY OF A DESK

DESK, n. table set, but not for feasting
cage of the horned knees
house of hope hobbled
barnacle, tank
incubator of wind and sighs
reliquary
aborted beach, unrisen garden,
    unfruited wood

Yesterday I found written in the grain of the wood four words: "You will join them." Today I looked again and only managed to pick out one word: "You."

Four words, then one. This is the promised sign. I have a few days to put my affairs

in order. Before then, it behooves me to record something of the curious history of this
desk or, I should say, the history of the
curious occupants of this desk.

My sources are as follows: (a) hearsay
(80%) (b) official documents (four) (c) a
departmental memo accounting for sudden
slumps in cataloging productivity (one:
1958 annual summation).

Here goes:

Sid Gravina. 1955–58. Mr. Gravina was a
quiet man, unobtrusive except for his green
eyeshade and plastic sleeves. "Meticulous
worker." In April 1958, he confessed to Mr.
Srb, his supervisor, that he had committed
murder, "not manslaughter—murder, murder with malice aforethought, subtle malice—not on the books." (Srb's verbatim
report.) Mr. Gravina had gone to the police,
the police had not believed him, yet he felt
he couldn't go on as if nothing had happened. Mr. Srb refused to accept his resigna-
tion but relieved Mr. Gravina of his duties
for one week (combination sick and personal leave).

Mr. Gravina returned from his leave as if
nothing had happened. His output ("quan-
tity and quality of work") was unaffected
for two months. This, in spite of half-hourly
trips to the lavatory to wash his hands (with-

147

out turning on the water). In September 1958, Mr. Gravina produced the longest chain of paper clips in library history. It reached from the main catalog room to the outer door of the building, where it extended three inches into the street. This chain was his "crime and its retribution," Mr. Gravina explained, "this—the actual noose." During this month, Mr. Gravina explained to anyone who would listen that his desk traveled at night, and displayed tread marks on the floor to prove it. After a flurry of poisoned notes, Mr. Gravina was permanently relieved of his responsibilities and recommended to a doctor's care. Not a ripple from him since.

Ada Nog. December 1958–May 1959. One-time harpsichordist. Spinster. Kept to herself. Claimed she had lupus after four months as archivist. Prolonged absence required a doctor's notice and no doctor agreed to lupus. She did have some sort of skin condition, some sort of nervous rash. After an uneventful day at work, Miss Nog put on her wrap, said goodnight, went home and put her head in the oven. No explanation offered or sought.

Shall I sing a song for you, Ada Nog?
A toast
to a most
unsavory roast.

Unfeeling? How's this?

> Death, break the stone loaf
>   for her hunger who
>   never tasted wine . . .

That better? Less punch, nicer sentiment. Slant's prettier on the page, too. What's the trade-off? Truth. Don't kid yourself, you'd sing the same two tunes for me. Simultaneously. Like the twin taps of the faucet, you'd run hot and cold from the one mouth. I don't know what the word "love" means. Is it some sort of hopeful incantation like "abracadabra"? Does it mean anything at all?

I am a bitter man, I am a lonely man, I am a most hungry man.

I wish to be buried with my desk. Why not? There's an established form for it, an analogue, a "ship burial" in which a ship is used as a tomb, often covered by a burial mound. I read that somewhere. I read a lot. Reading is a hunger with me.

My mind wanders lately.

There seems to be a war on.

Now I have written all I know about this desk, all that I know I know. I think of my predecessors at times and wonder: Is it the man that makes the desk or is it the desk that makes the man? Is this a desk at all or something else—a fine dappled horse, say, stalled under a spell of double enchantment?

What are these rumblings I hear? Shall I open the third drawer a crack and put my ear to the source of the sound? Is it a voice? Or an ear—some sort of recording device? Does the drawer report everything that goes on during the day? Everything? That Mr. Mac-Finster, our new supervisor, has been seen feeling the filing clerks under cover of the open catalog trays. At any rate, I have seen him. Frisking for stolen paper clips, maybe? Maybe. Let's be charitable.

Before the voice from the empty third drawer begins again, before the clickings, the mumbled obscenities, the curses, I hereby state what I must do, what I mean to do. I am going to stuff a wad in its mouth.

Remember me, remember me.

Ernest Coke
April 1969

A month later I had succeeded Ernest Coke.

I spilled everything I could into the empty third drawer, slamming it shut with a vigor that surprised me. By then I wasn't feeling too well, ears ringing with the echoes I had roused, my hands slick with some secretion—fear?

I was about to scram when I turned around to see what MacFinster was up to. He was in close conference with someone, someone terribly familiar. No chance of barging in to announce my indisposition.

Funny . . . something so familiar about . . . Who could it be? I glanced twice to make sure. There he was—in paste-on whiskers, muttonchop sideburns, a cheap disguise. He was wearing a maroon smoking jacket with heart-shaped lapels. He was smiling pleasantly at MacFinster inside the glass enclosure.

"Mr. Henken! Oh, Mr. Henken!" MacFinster rose and tapped on the plate partition. "I want you to meet our systems analyst. Would you come in, please?"

As I approached, I heard MacFinster explaining, "Mr. Henken is our specialist in ephemera and fugitive mat—"

I took one close look to confirm my wildest guess. No question about it: it *was* Dr. Grey. I shifted into reverse.

Home! Home to bed!

●

Trapped between myself and my mirror, I cannot run. It is better to lie between sheets, close to the horizontal, all fight gone, taking whatever comes.

I cut my hands to reach you, Meg. You've got to stick by me now.

They came in without knocking. Miss Kay ushered Meg into the room, indicating a place for her to sit on the edge of the bed. That done, she withdrew without a word.

Meg wore a navy blue coat, thrown over a gown that fell in long folds from her neck. She looked much as if she were only waiting for her escort, when she would sail forth on his arm, transformed for a ball. Her hair was freshly washed and brushed. There was a rare flush of anticipation in her cheeks, a soft amber light in her eyes.

She had come to say goodnight, I knew.

I stared at her blankly. You never see your own face in dreams, but she had my face on. Try as I might to soften my fixed stare, I knew my gaze to be cold, disbelieving, hard.

"How do you feel? As if I don't know . . ." She took my hand in hers.

"I feel with my fingers. Why? How do you feel?" I repeated without thought.

"You should have spent more time with whatshername Marysue or whatever, instead of rushing back to loveless me." She winked and moistened her lips with a glistening tongue.

"I wanted so much to help you, Meg. Can you believe that?"

"Maybe. But, me—I'm not an anagram. M–E–G—that's all—not G–E–M or any other twist. I'm what I seem, any idiot could tell that. Unteachable, but no mystery. It's people like you who make puzzles of themselves. Me, I'm perfectly straightforward, nothing hidden, no skin, in fact. You can read me like an open book. There's nothing to catching hold of me—"

So saying, she dove under the bed. For the time it took me to blink, she disappeared.

She reappeared, perfectly resettled on my desk chair.

"Let's see—what'll I write today? December what? But *you* must know the date, the same attached to the day—it's a charm against———— We try not to say those words in this house." She laughed mirthlessly, turning over a fresh page in my diary. *My* diary!

"That's enough—that settles it! That's mine—not yours! You've no right—" I shouted, whipping my blankets back and springing from the bed. I nearly fell over the chair, wanting so much to get my hands on her, to shake her to bits, to dust.

But the chair was empty. A fine veneer of dust lay unruffled over desk and chair. On my dresser, a row of wig stands I hadn't noticed before. They are faceless. And the fact is—I haven't kept a diary since the most sensitive days of my adolescence, back ten years or more.

Meg, Meg, why have you left me alone?

●

But she hasn't left—yet. I must have the last word. It's time to settle accounts, to sum things up, Meg and I. The sun is in my window; it will be a red day. I am wide awake.

From the floor above I hear the rattling of dishes, steps, shouts, drains, the first morning sounds. The radiator gives off something sweet, ether perhaps. The pipes choke with messages, love messages, laughter, screams. The screaming begins. . . . Neal Busch is in the whirly bird. He is writing *Good Morning* with the tail of his helicopter somewhere high above the traffic of the city. Teeth chattering, rising and falling, brave fellow, carry on! Never look back or down. . . .

It is time to wake Meg.

I leave the room, take a few steps down the hall, then press myself, heart pounding, against that silent door.

About the Author

A. G. Mojtabai was born in Brooklyn in 1937. She graduated from Antioch College in 1958 with a B.A. in philosophy and a minor in mathematics.

Soon after graduation, Ms. Mojtabai married and moved to Iran, where she lived with her husband in a large extended family. They later moved to Karachi, Pakistan, and then to Lahore.

When she returned to the United States, Ms. Mojtabai did graduate work at Columbia University, receiving an M.A. in philosophy in 1968 and an M.S. in Library Science in 1970. She lectured in philosophy for two years at Hunter College and is now a librarian at City College. Ms. Mojtabai lives in New York City with her daughter; she is at work on a new novel.